CJ

BOOKS BY FLEUR FERRIS

Risk
Black
Wreck
Found

FOUND

FLEUR FERRIS

RANDOM HOUSE AUSTRALIA

A Random House book
Published by Penguin Random House Australia Pty Ltd
Level 3, 100 Pacific Highway, North Sydney NSW 2060
www.penguin.com.au

Penguin
Random House
Australia

First published by Random House Australia in 2018

Addresses for the Penguin Random House group of companies can be found at
global.penguinrandomhouse.com/offices.

A catalogue record for this
book is available from the
NATIONAL
LIBRARY   National Library of Australia
OF AUSTRALIA

ISBN: 978 0 14378 432 6

Cover images © Reilika Landen / Arcangel and Dorota Gorecka / Trevillion
Images
Cover design by Christabella Designs
Internal design by Midland Typesetters, Australia
Typeset in 13.5/15.9 pt Perpetua by Midland Typesetters, Australia
Printed in Australia by Griffin Press, an accredited ISO AS/NZS 14001:2004
Environmental Management System printer

Penguin Random House Australia uses papers that are natural, renewable and
recyclable products and made from wood grown in sustainable forests. The logging
and manufacturing processes are expected to conform to the environmental
regulations of the country of origin.

For all the farm-raised kids of the world,
which just so happens to include my three daughters,
Zoe, Tia and Eve Ferris.

Also for David.

ONE
BETH

When Jonah kisses me I forget about everything else. Who knows about us, who doesn't, telling my father . . . Jonah pulls away and I'm left breathless and smiling-silly into his clear blue eyes. Who knew falling in love turned your brain to mush?

'So you're doing it now? *Before* karate?' Jonah says.

'Yes.' I laugh at the look of terror on his face. 'It'll be fine.'

'You do realise I'm training with him in a couple of hours? It'd only take one swift kick to the head.'

I raise my eyebrows and smirk.

'What?' Jonah says. 'He could kill me. Easily.'

'He'd never do that. He'd go to jail,' I say. 'If he was going to kill you, I think he'd wait until he could make it look like an accident.'

'Oh, Jesus. Survival camp.' Jonah groans. 'I'd forgotten about that. He nearly destroyed me last year and I wasn't even with his daughter then. Oh man, I don't know about this.'

'You mean about us?'

'No, I'm certain about us. I've never been more certain.' He pushes a strand of hair away from his eye. 'I mean about telling Bear. Fuck. Why can't you have a normal father? One who watches footy and drinks beer and mows the lawn on Saturday.'

'He does do those things.'

'Yeah, while he sharpens knives and does push-ups.'

I laugh as I lean back against the twisting trunk of the fig tree, which, for the past six Thursdays, we've kissed behind before going our separate ways. Jonah places his hands on my hips and pulls me closer.

'Knowing Bear, he already knows.' Jonah lowers his voice. 'He's probably crouched in the tree above us.'

Even though it's a joke we both look up.

Dad works for Parks and Wildlife in the building across the road, while Jonah's mum works at the post office on the other side of the gardens. Even though I could stay in town and walk to karate, Dad insists that I meet him at work. He leaves early, we go home and have dinner, then we drive back into town for training. I'd much rather just stay in town, but Dad doesn't want me 'loitering on the streets'.

I'd call it hanging out with friends, but making normal everyday things sound like criminal acts is one of Dad's many talents. Usually I'd be on the school bus and almost home by now, so even though it's short, I cherish this hour after school with Jonah each Thursday.

Of course, I'm not scared of Dad like the guys at school are. I'll be relieved when he knows about Jonah. Keeping secrets is hard work. You're always nervous, sometimes lying, forever covering things up . . . Besides, it's near impossible to keep secrets in this place. With only seven thousand people in the entire town, everyone seems to know everything about everyone, sometimes before the people involved even know. Jonah and I are the worst kept secret; half the kids at school suspect us and the other half already know for sure. Deni may be a remote little town in the middle of the New South Wales rice flats, but that doesn't stop news spreading like a crop fire on a windy summer's day.

Jonah leans to the side and looks over at my dad's car. He jerks his head back behind the tree.

'Holy shit. He's there already. He'll see me. He's gonna know before you tell him. I am *so* dead.'

I laugh at Jonah freaking out.

Dad is as disciplined and as strict as a drill sergeant. He's six-foot-six, heavily muscled and has a shaved head. These things alone intimidate the guys at school, but since we've been dating, that intimidation has ramped up to full-blown fear for Jonah.

A white van with dark windows turns into the street as I lean around the tree to take a peek. The van pulls up in the middle of the road, blocking my view of Dad and the car.

'Go now, while the van's there.' I can't believe our luck. Thank you, wonderful van driver – our hero.

Jonah kisses me on the lips. 'Good luck,' he says. 'Ring me if it turns ugly and you need me. I'm happy to be there.' He searches my eyes.

'It'll be fine. You go, I'll see you later at training.'

The truth is I have no idea how my dad will react to me having a boyfriend. He likes Jonah, he's one of his best students, plus I'm seventeen, so it shouldn't be too big a deal. But Dad can be way too over-protective sometimes. I wasn't allowed to have any social media accounts until last year. Then, when he finally let me online, he imposed strict rules. I'm never to put my real name, Elizabeth Miller, on any account. I use KarateKidBeth, which I know is cheesy, but I couldn't think of anything cool at the time and was just stoked to be finally joining the rest of the world. I'm not allowed to 'friend' anyone I don't know personally or put photos of Mum or Dad on there, and my settings have to be private. If I break any of the rules, I'll be cut off from the wi-fi at home and my phone will be confiscated. It totally sucks. None of my friends have restrictions like that.

I watch Jonah jog away; tall, athletic, sun-kissed skin and shoulders to die for. A smile plays on my lips as I smooth my hair and straighten my uniform. When I step out from behind the tree the white van pulls away. The wheels screech just a little as it speeds down the road and turns left, out of sight.

I look up and down the street then squint to see inside the dark windows of our car, but they're all empty.

Dad's gone.

TWO
JONAH

Jonah jogs away from Beth without looking back.

The Waring Gardens are the main feature of Deni and located right in the centre of town. All the local businesses scramble for office space overlooking the parklands. The park hosts an abundance of trees, shrubs and flowers. There are rotundas covered in creepers, fountains and statues, but the main feature of the gardens is the large lagoon and footbridge, which brings in as many people as it does waterbirds.

Jonah heads towards the peacock aviary to run around the lagoon, but then he changes track and decides to cross the water by going over the bridge. The foliage is thicker around the lake. The plants with dark green leaves and orange flowers will give him better cover. Once he's over the other side and certain he's out of Bear's line of sight, Jonah slows to a walk and finds Warra sitting on one of the park benches, hunched over his biology textbook. His backpack and bike are lying on the grass beside him.

Like lots of kids in Deni, Warra travels everywhere by bike. He lives two kays out of town so often hangs around after school if he has sport on in the evening. He doesn't see Jonah at first because of the thick, dark curls that fall over his eyes.

Jonah smiles. Warra's a good mate. When Jonah was training for the Karate National Championships, Warra held the bag for hours and asked for nothing in return. He said he just really wanted someone from Deni to win. That's one of the best things about this town. Everyone wants to see the locals succeed. They do whatever it takes to help them achieve their goal, and when they do, the whole town is proud of them.

Warra finally looks up when Jonah plonks his bag down on the bench. Jonah lets out a long sigh and shakes his head. Warra sucks at the straw of his thickshake and puts it down beside him.

'Everyone knows, man. Bear's gonna find out sooner or later, and when he does you're dead meat.' Warra's red school jumper slips off the seat and onto the ground, but he leaves it there.

Jonah sits down. 'Beth's telling him now,' he says, nerves tightening his gut. He pulls out his phone and types Beth a quick message to wish her luck.

'Before training?' Warra stares at Jonah, eyes wide.

'I know.' Jonah shakes his head again. 'My thoughts exactly.' He presses send.

'Whoa.' Warra whistles though his teeth. 'You're either the bravest or most brainless dude I know.'

'I'm hearing that a bit lately.'

'No wonder. There's a reason she's never had a boyfriend before, why no one else has dared to go there. Can't you hook up with someone else? Someone less . . . life threatening?' Warra half laughs, but Jonah can see he's also half serious.

'I don't want anyone else. It's different with Beth. She's worth all of this trouble. If Bear wants to kick my head in at karate tonight, so be it.' Jonah speaks confidently, but inside he's dreading going to training. He's already thinking up possible excuses why he can't go.

Warra holds out his hand. Jonah shakes it. 'Good luck, man. If anything happens, I'll stand up for you.'

'Yeah?' Jonah says. Warra's skinny and almost a head shorter than Jonah. He could never take on Bear, but Jonah doesn't doubt that he'd stand up for him anyway. He and Warra go way back. Warra's the kind of guy you can tell something to and know it won't go any further. At school he's quiet, but everyone likes him. No one gives him shit.

'Absolutely. I'll tell the police everything I know. Then, if they promise to protect me, I'll agree to

8

give evidence at your murder trial. I'll even say nice things about you at your funeral.'

He also makes Jonah laugh.

'You'd do that for me? Thanks, man. I knew I could count on you.'

'Always.' Warra cracks a broad smile.

'Anyway, I'd better get going,' Jonah says, checking his watch. It's almost four. 'Mum will be waiting.'

'Yeah. Enjoy these last few moments. Maybe get something nice to eat. Treat yourself.'

'Fuck off,' Jonah says, before heading across the road towards his mum's building.

THREE
BETH

The car doors are locked, so I stand and wait. Dad must have ducked back into his office. When I get sick of standing I lean against the passenger door with my feet on the edge of the gutter and take out my phone. There's a message and photo from Willow.

Sprung! It's accompanied by a picture of Jonah and me kissing in the park just now.

I snort a laugh as I write back.

Pervert!

Willow and I have been best friends since preschool. One day, to learn about opposites, we were asked to team up with the person in class who was most unlike ourselves. Most girls teamed up with boys and vice versa, but we turned to each other and smiled. We were a perfect opposite match.

She's fair-skinned and I'm tanned. She's small, I'm tall. She's soft and curvy, I'm hard and straight up and down. She's artsy and wants to be a famous actor and I don't have a creative bone in my body, and yet somehow we complement each other. Willow was the Yin to my Yang back then and still is today. I can't imagine life without her.

Willow's face lights up on my screen as she calls. I pick up immediately. She bypasses hellos.

'You are so dead,' she says.

'Relax, I'm just about to tell him. I'm at the car waiting for him right now.'

'Really? Don't you and Jonah have karate training with him this arvo?'

'Yes. It'll be fine. What's Dad going to do?'

'God, I might take up karate just so I can come and watch.'

I laugh. 'Have *you* decided what *you're* going to do?'

Willow exaggerates a groan. 'No. Yes. I don't know. I guess I have to . . . I just feel bad because it's not like we're fighting, and I like spending time with him. I just don't feel the zing, you know?'

'The zing's important.'

'Yeah, it's not right without it.'

'How do you think he'll take it?'

'Ugh . . . That's why I'm stalling. I don't want to hurt him, but I'm already doing that by avoiding being alone with him. He knows something's up.'

'You want me to stay at your place tomorrow night? We could overdose on Netflix and mango ice-cream with chocolate sprinkles.'

'Really? What about Jonah? If Bear doesn't kill or maim him tonight, you might be allowed to go to Audrey's seventeenth together.'

'Will you be going?'

'Not if I dump Sam. He's better friends with her and it'd just be awkward. I wouldn't want to ruin her night.'

'Well, if you do, Jonah can go to Audrey's to check Sam's okay and I'll come to your house to check you're okay.'

'Are you sure? It could be your first night of wild, public coupledom.'

I throw my head back and laugh. 'As if. And yes, of course I'm sure. Audrey wouldn't want you home on your own all miserable. And besides, Mum's going because she's friends with Audrey's mum. There will be no wild displays of public coupledom while she's watching.'

'Okay. I feel better now. You always make me feel better. Always, always, always.' Willow sucks in a huge breath. 'Right. I'll be strong. I'll do it. I'll tell Sam tonight.'

'Okay. And I'll tell Dad.'

Willow laughs. 'I'm not sure which is worse. Anyway, good luck. I've gotta fly. You're the best, Beth. Love ya.' Willow makes two quick kiss sounds into the phone and hangs up.

Before I put my phone in my pocket I check the time. Dad's late. My gaze settles on the front door of his office building. I push off the car and take a few aimless paces up and down the footpath.

Then I see it.

Dad's backpack, lying on the road behind the car.

It's so unlike him to leave it there. Deni's a safe town. Even if someone saw it, they probably wouldn't take it. But still, Dad's not exactly lax about that kind of thing.

For a split second I worry that Dad saw us and took off after Jonah, but that's ridiculous. He wouldn't do that. He must have gone back into his office. Then I remember the van. Maybe there was some kind of emergency and someone needed help. Maybe he went with them.

I push open the heavy glass door of Dad's building and step into the reception area. The receptionist, Sally-Ann, looks up from her screen and smiles.

'Hey, Beth. I'm pretty sure your dad's already left for the day.'

'Hi, Sally-Ann,' I say. 'I saw him by the car just now but next minute he'd disappeared. I thought he might have come back in for something.'

'Oh. I didn't see him, but hang on, I'll check.' Sally-Ann picks up the phone and presses a button. 'Hello, is Bear back there?' she says. 'No, I saw him leave too, but Beth's here looking for him.' She pauses. 'Okay.' Sally-Ann hangs up. 'Sorry, Beth. No one saw him come back in.'

'Thanks for checking. I'll go back to the car and wait. Maybe he went down the road to the shops or something.' But even as I say it I know he didn't do that. I have his backpack.

When I reach the car I place the backpack on the bonnet and open it. Inside the main compartment is Dad's jumper and a lunch box. I unzip the front pocket and find Dad's phone and wallet. He definitely didn't go to the shops. I retrieve my phone from my bag and call Mum.

'Hey, Beth.'

'Hi, Mum.' I pause. 'How's things?'

'Good. Is everything all right?'

'I don't know where Dad is. I mean, he was here, but then he disappeared and his bag was on the ground like he left in a hurry. I just checked inside with Sally-Ann and he's not there either.'

'What do you mean? He was there and then he disappeared?'

'Well, I saw him by the car waiting for me, then this van drove by and stopped in front of him. When the van left, Dad was gone. If he went with the van, why wouldn't he take his bag? It was on the road behind the car. It just seems a bit weird.'

'Where are you now?' There's a tightness in Mum's voice that wasn't there before. She sounds stressed. I can hear her walking.

'Waiting at the car.'

'Walk away from it.'

'What?'

'Walk towards Napier Street and stay on the phone. I'm on my way.'

'Mum, what's going on?'

'Just do as I say, Beth. It's important.'

Mum's footsteps break into a run. A door slams, then her car roars to life.

'Why?'

'Beth, just do it. I'm already in town, I won't be long.'

'But, Mum . . .' I pick up my pace and don't look back. Mum's panic pulses through me, an electric current from her to me.

When I reach Napier Street I continue around the corner then dawdle up and down because it feels better than standing still. A few minutes later Mum pulls up on the road beside me.

'What's wrong?' I ask as I get into the car.

Mum ignores my question. As soon as I close the door she takes off. We turn right at the end of the street and head in the opposite direction to home.

'Where are we going?'

Mum pulls into Rams Oval, which is empty at this time of day. She drives towards the clubrooms and parks near the main building.

'Get out.'

I do as she says and follow her to stand near the clubrooms.

'Tell me everything you saw,' Mum says.

'*What's* going on? Why are you being so weird and –'

'Elizabeth,' Mum cuts me off. She only ever calls me that when I'm in trouble. 'It's important. Tell me what you saw.'

'Dad was near the car, then a white van pulled up in front of him and drove off. Dad was gone.'

'Where were you?'

'In the park.'

'Were you with anyone?'

I feel my face flush red.

'Beth, were you with anyone?'

'No. I was on my own. What is this?'

'Did they see you?'

'Who?'

'The people in the van.'

'No.'

Mum walks back to the car and grabs Dad's bag. She unzips the front, takes out his phone and turns it off. Then she turns off her phone and holds them both in one hand.

'Give me your phone,' she says.

'Why?' Is she going to check my messages? To see if I'm lying about being alone?

'Just do it.' Her voice is sharp.

I glare at her as I unzip my bag and retrieve my phone. On the screen is a message from Jonah.

Good luck! xx

'Turn it off.'

I do as she says, relieved she won't see Jonah's message.

Mum holds out her free hand for the phone. I pass it over, frowning, worried . . .

She walks towards the nearest bin and tosses them in before reaching down to move some of the rubbish around to cover them.

'What are you doing?' I screech.

'Get back in the car.'

Tears prick my eyes. Has she gone crazy?

'Why would you do that? You're scaring me,' I say.

'I'll get you a new phone,' she says.

I get back into the car.

Mum reverses out and drives back to the main road. We're heading towards home.

'Where are we going now? Home?'

'We can't talk in the car,' Mum says.

'What are you on about?'

'I'll explain everything as soon as I can,' she says.

'Why can't we talk in the car? What's going on?'

Mum doesn't answer, so I look away from her out the passenger window. Soon we're out of town and I'm staring at nothing but the vast open plains. Anger builds and simmers inside me. Mum seemed fine this morning. Normal.

Our farm is fifty kays out of town and now Mum's speeding.

'I'm sorry, Beth. I'm so very sorry,' she says, shaking her head. She looks at me. 'Just pray to God I'm wrong.'

My chest tightens. It's not her words that are so disturbing, it's the heaviness of her tone. My next breath snags in my throat. Mum goes to speak but stops, like she's trying to find the best way to tell me bad news.

I think about the van. Has Dad gone to help someone? Or maybe an animal needed rescuing, he's rushed off to do that before. Or is he in some kind of trouble?

But the phones. That part doesn't make sense . . .

My thoughts flip around to every hypothetical my brain can conjure up, but I can't join the dots.

I look at Mum: her focus, her white knuckles, her clenched jaw and constant checking of mirrors. I've never seen her like this before. She's stressed . . . or scared . . . or both. My skin prickles with fear.

She just said she's sorry.

So very sorry.

What is she sorry about?

The road is straight but we're going so fast I'm getting uncomfortable. Not because it feels danger-ous, but because Mum never speeds. My hand feels for the door handle and my fingers tighten around it.

'Mum, you're speeding,' I say.

Mum glances down at the speedometer, then her

eyes flick back up to the rear-view mirror. 'Mary, mother of God,' she mutters. 'Hold on.'

She brakes, then swerves off the main road onto a disused dirt track. My hip and shoulder slam into the passenger door.

'Mum, what the hell?'

'We're being followed.'

'By who? Why? What's going on?'

I turn to look out the back window.

'No one's there,' I say.

'Yes, they are. I can guarantee it. Keep watching.'

We're flying and dust plumes up behind the car.

Then I see a familiar white van turn into the dirt road behind us.

'Who are they?' I ask. 'Is Dad with them? Why don't we stop and see what they want?'

'I know I sound paranoid, but we can't talk in the car. I don't know if it's bugged.'

Despite my nerves I laugh because it's ludicrous. We're the most boring family on the planet. Who would bug our car?

'I'll fill you in when we're outside. When it's safe to talk. I know you're scared, I know you're confused, but there are things you don't know about us. Things that I can't tell you right now, not here in this car.'

Mum turns off the dirt track. We are on the Frankels' property now, our neighbours. Their land is on the opposite side of the main road to ours.

We drive into the trees and over a culvert that crosses the main channel that runs through the Frankels', Youngs' and our place. I take another look out the rear window but can't see the van because the trees are so thick here. Mum pulls the car off the road and we roll into a small shed out of sight. Mum cuts the engine.

'Get out of the car.'

I do as she says.

'Keep with me and do everything I say.'

Our eyes meet. I nod.

We run back through the trees until we reach the channel. Mum goes straight over the bank and into a thicket of dry cumbungi reeds. I stop. There's a bit of muddy water in the bottom of the channel. I'm not going in there.

'C'mon, Beth,' Mum commands. 'You've been in channels before.'

'Yeah, in gumboots.'

'It's just a bit of water.'

'And slime and leeches.'

Mum looks towards the road in the direction the van will come. 'Hurry, Elizabeth!'

I do as she says. Freezing water fills my school shoes and seeps up my pants to my knees. The cumbungi stops me from sinking too far into the mud that sucks at my feet, threatening to swallow my shoes. I follow Mum deeper into the reeds, the ground bubbling with every step. It stinks.

'There'd better be a really good reason for this,' I mutter.

Mum stops and pulls me down, out of sight. The reeds are so tall and thick I can't see through them but I hear the van in the distance. Mum places a finger over her lips. Then she pulls out her Walther P22. My eyes pop at the sight of it. Where did that come from? As far as I know Mum never carries her gun in town. A thousand new questions race through my mind about the people in the van and what they might want. How do they know us and how do my parents – the straightest parents in town, or so I thought – know them?

I hold my breath, heart hammering, eyes wide. Normally, seeing Mum with a pistol is no shock. She's good with guns. We all are because Dad's involved in running both the local pistol club and the clay target shooters club. But seeing Mum squatting down in thick cumbungi with her Walther drawn while a mysterious white van approaches is so scary I could choke.

What will they do if they find us? What has Mum so afraid that she would need to carry her gun? Is she going to shoot them? Are they going to shoot us?

FOUR
JONAH

Jonah stands outside the post office and waits for his mum. Before long Ida steps outside.

'Hi, love, you ready?' she says.

Jonah shrugs.

'Where's your sister?'

'Haven't seen her.'

'She'd better not be with —'

Before Ida finishes her sentence Carly strides up the street towards them, pink hair sailing in the wind like a TV commercial. Carly smiles like the cat who just ate the canary.

'How was your day at school?' Ida asks, eyeing Carly suspiciously.

'Yeah, good.' Jonah nods.

'Mine was great,' says Carly.

Jonah looks at his sister. He notices her lipstick, the sparkle in her eye, her swagger. She was like this when she was with Trent. All stupid and gooey about everything. The rumours must be true, and Ida must have heard them too. Carly looks at Jonah's raised eyebrows and winks.

No way.

The olds are going to spit it. It actually makes Jonah's Bear problem pale into insignificance.

Trent is a local, three years older than Carly, and a bad influence to say the least. When they started dating Carly fell hard. She went right off the rails and did stupid things to be with him. She got caught sneaking out, going to parties she wasn't allowed to be at and smoking pot. Then Trent smashed up the front door of the hospital one night when he was off his face on ice. He punched on with the cops, got arrested and charged, lost his job as a road worker at the council and was pretty much totally shamed by the whole town. He disappeared for a few months and Jonah's parents hoped they'd never see him again. But now he's back and Carly's like this again.

Carly sits in the front seat on the way home. Normally she complains about Mum's golden oldie channel, but today she sings along. Carly goes to singing lessons while Jonah's at karate, so she's always belting out song lyrics at the top of her lungs. Jonah has a good stash of earplugs in his room for when she practises at home.

Training is at five thirty but Ida insists they go home first to have dinner, even though it's early. Really it's so Carly isn't left to hang around in town for another hour and a half. Less time to spend with guys like Trent.

'You two start while I get changed,' Ida says as she heads to her room.

Jonah goes to the fridge and takes out the leftover casserole. Carly places three bowls on the counter, humming a tune.

'What's up with you?' Jonah lowers his voice. 'Why are you so happy?'

'What's up with you?' Carly whispers back. 'Why are you shitting your pants?'

Jonah snorts a laugh. Carly could always read him like a book. 'Is it that obvious? Beth's gonna tell Bear about us this afternoon.' He glances at the time on the microwave while Carly sits down at the table. 'She's probably already done it.'

'Holy shitballs.' Carly leans back in her seat. 'She's telling him before training?'

'God, I wish everyone would stop saying that.'

'Well, mate, seriously. We're talking about the same guy who threw a knife and hit a five-foot goanna between the eyes when it was sitting twenty-five metres away. Then he cooked it and made everyone eat it.'

'It was survival camp, Carly. Catching your own food is part of the experience.'

Carly rolls her eyes. 'My point is he can knife throw like some kind of circus pro. You can only do that shit if you practise fifty million times a day. I mean, who sits out on a farm in the middle of fuck-knows-where throwing knives all day? It's creepy if you ask me.'

'He works in town, you douche. And he runs karate classes after work, so he can't be out there throwing knives all day.'

Carly gives him a look. 'He fits it in somewhere. Maybe he throws knives late at night.'

Jonah swallows. Carly always points out things he doesn't think of. What kind of man does do that? Jonah hears his mum's footsteps down the other end of the house and remembers what he had to ask Carly.

'I heard you're back with Trent. Is it true?'

Carly smiles and nods.

'Carls, he's bad news.'

'He's clean now. He wants his job back and he has to be clean to work there. They do tests.'

'I just hope you know what you're doing.'

'Same to you, little brother.'

Ida walks back into the kitchen in her active-wear, runners and a hoodie. 'I might wait and eat with your father tonight. Cheryl brought in a tray of doughnuts, so we all had afternoon tea.'

Ida eats like a bird. Jonah bets she won't even have dinner when his dad gets home.

Jonah and Carly finish their meals and make small talk. When Jonah glances at the clock again it's time to go. He takes a deep breath, trying to calm his nerves. He gets into the back seat without a fight, even though Carly had the front on the way home. He sits, silent, grateful for Carly's singing. The calm before the Bear-storm. Jonah looks out the window, hoping he doesn't throw up his dinner.

FIVE
BETH

The van gets closer. The revs drop as it slows to cross the culvert. It crawls by and the revs pick up as it leaves, looping back up towards the main road.

I exhale. Is Dad in that van? If he is we need to rescue him. What are they going to do to him?

Mum turns to me. 'We're going to be okay,' she says. 'Your father and I have prepared for this.'

Using the channel as cover, Mum watches the van until it's out of sight.

'Our car can't have had a tracker on it. They would have stopped if it did. This gives us more time.'

I stare at Mum. What have my parents done?

'We're going to travel along this channel.' Mum points. 'There's enough water in it to cover our tracks. It's hard going, but your father and

I have done it before so we know it's possible. When we get near the road we'll have to keep our heads down, but other than that we're pretty well covered. Oh, and out here our voices travel, so it's probably best not to talk too much. I promise I'll explain everything when we get there.'

'Get where?'

'A safe place, you'll see.'

'Shouldn't we call the police?'

Mum looks at me for a moment like she's searching for the right words.

'Yes, we do need help . . . but we'll bring in the police who are specially trained for this kind of thing. We don't want any harm to come to our local guys.'

'What kind of thing?' I ask. Why can't she just say? And who is *we*? Are there others involved?

'Mum, what have you done?'

'It all happened a long time ago,' she says, glancing over her shoulder. 'It's best if you save your questions for when we get there.'

Ahhh, the magical safe place, I think. *Of course.*

Mum starts walking. I follow. It's impossible to move very fast because our feet keep sinking into the mud. The grey sludge is streaked with a mustard-coloured slime and I hope I don't fall in. My feet are so cold they hurt. Our footprints disappear behind us and I try not to think about the concentration of leeches in such small amounts of water.

Our farm is a long rectangular shape with the longest side running along the main road, Caldwell Lane. Before reaching our place there's the Youngs' farm, and the Frankels own the land on the opposite side of the road. The main channel is owned by the government and snakes through all of our properties to smaller feeder channels that provide irrigation to the crops.

As we trudge towards the Youngs' place my body thrums with adrenaline and fear. Questions flood my mind but for now I must focus on reaching the 'safe place', wherever that is. If we follow this main channel we'll eventually reach our own property, but surely we're not going to walk all the way. Maybe the safe place is somewhere on the Youngs' farm? Maybe it's their place? They're away on holiday at the moment, but they wouldn't mind us going inside and using their phone in an emergency. As long as we take off our shoes.

Mum stops. We've reached a section of channel with no cumbungi.

'Beth, we're going to have to move faster for this next part. If they come back along the road they can see right down the length of the channel and we don't have any cover. It's about one kay.'

I swallow. I'm not sure I can go any faster. My feet are already numb and they'll sink into the mud even more when there's no roots to hold us up.

'You okay?' Mum says.

I nod. But no. No. I'm not okay. I'm standing in freezing mud while God-knows-who is hunting us.

Mum steps out of the water onto the dry section of the channel, careful not to leave footprints. She lies flat against the bank of the channel and crawls up on her elbows. She peers over, then scrambles back down.

'The road's clear. Let's go.'

She starts running and I follow. It's slow and awkward. My left shoe is sucked off my foot and disappears as the mud folds over the top of it. I stop. Mum looks back.

'My shoe.'

'Leave it.'

I do as she says. Her hand moves to her hip where her gun is and rests there for a moment. She stumbles, goes down on one knee, then she's up and running again. Our pace is slow and cumbersome, only just faster than a walk.

I stumble too and my hands hit the mud. I recover, push myself back up and stay close to Mum. My heart thuds hard in my chest from the work of the run.

One hundred metres.

My legs are heavy. My thighs burn. I'm fit but this is hard work. I concentrate on my breathing, my posture, and I pump my arms trying to find a better rhythm. I breathe in through my nose, out through my mouth. The mud sucks at my feet with every step and I realise there is less resistance on my foot with no shoe. I stomp down hard with my right foot and let the mud take my other shoe. I'm past caring about the slime, the stink, and the leeches. My concern is reaching the bridge before that van comes back. I notice Mum's hand keeps moving to her holster at her side, checking her gun is still there. She's breathing hard, arms pumping, focused.

Two hundred metres.

Three hundred metres.

Four hundred.

Almost halfway.

Mum stops. 'Shhh!'

I freeze and hold my breath.

'Hear that?' she whispers.

I do. A car engine.

Mum scrambles up the channel's bank, takes one look and flies back down. She doesn't have to say anything because the colour has drained from her face.

They're coming.

I look down at my bright red school jumper. I'm like a flag, screaming to be seen. But my shirt underneath it is white. That will stand out too.

'Lie down,' I say.

Mum knows what I'm thinking.

'You first. I'll make sure you're covered.'

I fall onto my back. The water seeps through my clothes, into my hair and ears. The cold takes my breath away. It's sheer pain. I try to think of something else but I can't. It's too overwhelming.

Mum pushes me down into the mud. As I sink the slush folds over the top of my body. Mum's hovering, smearing my face, leaving only my mouth and nose clear to breathe. The fear in her eyes chills me more than the freezing water. Then she disappears from view. Her hand grabs mine as she falls into the mud beside me and flails around to push herself deeper onto the floor of the channel.

We lie still, our fingers linked. I realise it's our only method of communication.

I listen to my heart pounding. The air going in and out of my lungs. Everything is amplified and makes me feel panicky. The cold is numbing my body now. I focus and try to calm my thoughts, slowing my erratic breathing.

I take in the clear blue of the sky above us. It's a perfect winter's day.

Still. Sunny. Peaceful. Things are going to be okay.

Three pelicans glide into view, serene and graceful. Their wings are spread wide, their legs drawn back while they ride the thermals. Watching them calms me down. My eyes follow them until they disappear. My breathing is now deep and even. Then the cold takes over and I can't stop my body from shaking. I can't think about anything except the icy water burning my skin. I try to focus on the blue again, but I can't. There is nothing but this awful coldness. How long do we have to lie here? How will we know when it's safe to move? My heart speeds up again.

I wonder about the temperature of the mud and how long my body can stay submerged in it before becoming hypothermic. Would it be six degrees? Seven or eight? I should know this. It's Dad's thing. Once a year, in the September school holidays, he takes kids out into the bush on survival camp and teaches them things like how to find water, what to eat and how to protect themselves from the elements. Basically, how to survive in their harsh environment. My friends say he's like Bear Grylls in *Man vs. Wild*, only bigger, madder and much scarier. It's why everyone calls him Bear. Most people don't even know his real name is Gregory.

Our family name is Miller. It's funny. Miller seems to be the town's generational name. Half of Deni are Millers or related to them, except us. We have the same name but we're not related to anyone else in town. We even share first names with other Millers here. There are three Elizabeth Millers, four Gregory Millers and two Lucy Millers, which is my mum's name.

I've always envied big families. Mum and Dad were both only children and all four of my grandparents died when I was a baby, so we have no living relatives. My friends talk about spending holidays with cousins, aunts and uncles. I'd love to have that.

I feel pressure on my hand and I think Mum is lifting her head to take a look. I've lost all sense of time. Has it been five minutes? Six? Ten? Then her face is in front of mine, mouthing to stay still while she checks the road. I'm startled by the sight of her. She's all mud except for her wild, terrified eyes. I try to stop my body shaking but I can't. A moment later she's back, digging out my arms and pulling me to my feet from the suction of the mud. Mum picks up her gun from the bank, shoves it into her holster, then we're running again. I'm stiff and awkward now. I try to focus on moving as quickly as possible, placing one leg in front of the other. I tell myself every step is one less to take. Soon we'll be at the safe place. The place where we can talk, the place where Mum will tell me everything. Hopefully the safe place is warm.

To distract myself, I try to come up with some theories about what's going on. What could my parents have done? Maybe they stumbled across something they weren't supposed to see. Something bad. A drug crop or lab and now they're after us. But if that had happened, wouldn't they have just called the police?

Dad has lots of guns in the safe at home. Maybe someone wants to steal them? But they took Dad, not his guns. Unless they need him to open the safe. That's a possibility. But then wouldn't they take him home? Why would they chase me and Mum? None of these ideas make sense.

My breathing is at a good rhythm and my body is warming up again. Mum powers on in front of me. She's super fit. I guess she has to keep up with Dad, and he's relentless. He never slackens off. If he's not at work or teaching martial arts, he's at the gun range or planning for the next survival camp. The thing is, he doesn't train to win competitions like other people do. He doesn't even let me compete in high-level comps. When I've wanted to he says, 'We don't need medals to make us feel good about ourselves. We do it for here,' and he taps his heart. But when Jonah recently won the National Championship for his category, Dad was so excited. Jonah's mum took a photo of him after the fight with Dad in the background. Jonah posted the photo on Instagram because he loved that Dad looked so proud of him. I thought it was cute but I told Jonah to take it down. Dad would be furious if he knew a photo of himself went up on social media.

We're almost at the bridge where the channel goes under Caldwell Lane. Then we'll be on the Youngs' property. Just after the bridge the channel bends to the left and runs down the Youngs' fence line, parallel with the road. It'll be easier to hide on that stretch. After that, the channel swings off to the right and into our property, heading away from Caldwell Lane. No one could possibly see us from the road then.

When we reach the bridge, I notice that the underside of it is covered in mud nests built by swallows. I guess we're not the only ones using it for cover and protection. I'm hoping Mum will take a break, give us five minutes' rest, but she doesn't. She's already making a dash for the next corner. In a fresh burst, she sprints, her feet plunging deep into the mud with every step. The water is getting deeper, making it harder and noisier to run.

Thirty metres.

Twenty metres.

Ten.

Then she's out of sight.

I follow and gasp with relief as I make it around the bend.

A low hum reaches my ears. I stop running and listen hard. A car is coming.

'Lie flat on this side of the bank,' Mum says, inching her way to the edge for a look. 'It's not them,' she says a moment later, collapsing to her knees.

I get ready to spring to my feet.

'We should flag them down. They could help us!'

'No!' Mum snaps. 'Stay down.'

'But they'd stop and help us.' My voice cracks. 'I want to get out of here.' Tears well up in my eyes.

Mum crouches down and places her hands on my shoulders.

'Elizabeth, listen to me, these people are here to kill us. It's personal and they will stop at nothing. They will kill our neighbours, our friends, the local police, anyone who helps us, anyone who gets in their way. We cannot involve anyone else. Do you understand?'

Terror strangles my words. Audrey's mum, Zoe, is a police officer. She's one of Mum's best friends and Audrey is one of mine. I try to swallow the lump in my throat as fat tears run down my cheeks.

'Beth, do you understand?' Mum presses.

'No. No, Mum, I don't understand. What have you done? Why is this happening?'

'It's something that happened before you were born. We lived a different life back then. But don't worry, we're prepared for today,' Mum says. 'We have things in place.'

'Oh, yeah, real prepared.' I slap the mud with my foot.

'C'mon, Beth, we don't have time for this.'

We trudge through the water, side by side, our feet sinking into the mud.

'Your dad and I were involved in a police operation years ago,' Mum says. 'It was in America. You were just a baby.'

'America?'

'Yes.' Mum hesitates before saying, 'You were born there.'

This news rocks me. I thought I was born in Sydney – that's what I'd always been told. Too many thoughts fly through my mind to process, but a discomforting sense of betrayal moves into my chest. On countless occasions I'd begged Mum and Dad about going to America for a holiday. I've always been fascinated by it, always wanted to go there. But when I told Mum I wanted to see the Grand Canyon, visit New York City, go to Disneyland and see the stars on the pavement in Hollywood, she'd brush it off and claim that she and Dad had no interest in America whatsoever. She said they'd never been there.

'You lied.' I can't help but spit the words. Fury swirls inside me.

Mum nods. 'Yes,' she says. There's no apology. Just 'yes'. Is that all she has to say?

I clench my jaw. And I was worried about hiding secrets.

'Something bad happened, something we never wanted to involve you in until we had no choice.'

'What?'

'Not now, Beth. I need to sit down with you to have this conversation.'

'Why?'

'Because you're going to need my full attention, and while we're out here I have to focus on getting you to safety.'

I protest, but she doesn't budge on her 'we have to wait' stance. We continue walking in silence. I don't know if I'm more angry, hurt or confused.

Moving at a slower pace, I'm soon cold again.

'How much further?' I ask.

'About two kays, maybe less.'

A normal two-kay walk is nothing, but in this wet, muddy channel it feels like a marathon.

We move through the Youngs' property, never leaving the channel, and finally enter our own farm. We pass the turkey nest, our largest dam, and follow the channel around a bend, wading through more cumbungi. It's much easier to walk where there are roots and weeds, but it's rough on my bare feet. Mum offers me her shoes but I refuse to take them.

Two spoonbills standing in the water take flight as we approach. They are my favourite of the many waterbirds on our farm. I know there will be ducks and pelicans in the turkey nest and the wedge-tailed eagle will be perched at the top of the dead tree that stands in the water. It's always there. Forever waiting. A calculated and patient hunter.

Walking up and over the bank would startle the rest of these birds into flight and I realise that could give away our location. If the guys in the van noticed, it would lead them straight to us. I can't help but think that we are their prey, being hunted. Are they too waiting patiently like the eagle? Watching for signs of movement?

We reach a junction where the main channel intersects our smaller feeder channel. The feeder channel turns into an enclosed pipe that takes the water across the main channel. Mum stops under the pipe.

'We have to move from this channel to that one.' Mum points to the feeder channel. 'It's risky. We'll be exposed and could be seen.'

I can see the issue. If we take the most direct route, we have to cross the road that runs down the side of one of our paddocks before dropping back into the smaller channel. If we go over the other bank, we're exposed for less time and distance, but we have to crawl through the feeder channel's enclosed pipe for about forty metres.

'I think we should go that way and crawl through the pipe,' I say.

Mum nods. 'I agree. We have an underground bunker at the base of the dry dam. That's where we're going. We can get in through another pipe about halfway down that way.'

She points towards the house.

'A bunker?' I say. 'Under the old dry dam?' It's hard to believe. I used to ride my motorbike around the walls of it like it was a velodrome. I've jumped my bike over the edge and into the basin a thousand times. Not once did I ever suspect anything could be under there.

'Yes, your dad built it especially. We can call for help from there and sit this out safely.'

'What about Dad?'

'Let's hope he's got away from those guys and is already there.'

Thinking Dad might be there gives me a fresh burst of energy. Being safe and getting warm and calling for help, it all sounds good. Mum can explain whatever it is that they've done and why we have an underground bunker. I still can't believe it. I imagine it's like a cement tank dug into the ground.

Before Dad worked for Parks he worked in emergency management. Over the years he's advised people from all over Australia about underground cyclone and fire shelters. Here in Deni we don't get cyclones and the flat, open landscape makes it possible to escape fires, so I've never heard of anyone with a bunker on their property.

The last leg is the hardest because we have to crawl on our hands and knees. If we stood up we'd be taller than the banks and visible from the road. I just want to get to the bunker. It's all I can think about now we're so close.

We stay low and edge our way along the feeder channel and finally we're there. A large black pipe that I've seen a million times before but never given a second thought to sticks out from the channel wall. There are pipes all over this farm. Every channel, every dam has them. Mum lifts the valve. Inside is another valve that she has to unscrew.

'The channel's not running now so water can't enter this pipe, but as a safeguard I want you to always screw in this stop so it's secure. If the dam fills while we're in the bunker, we'd be stuck down there.'

'Why would you put the bunker there then? Why not put it somewhere else?'

'If the stop is in then it doesn't matter, the dam will never fill. Dad chose the bottom of the basin as the entry point because it provides cover for us to get in and out. Plus a disused dam is the last place anyone would look and we needed a believable cover story for all the construction when we were building it. This dam has never held water, so we told the neighbours we were trying to fix it.'

'But what about in summer when the channels are running?' I ask.

'That's what the big stop is for,' Mum says as she points to the main channel stop. 'It's also why we never lease out the land that needs to be irrigated on this side of the channel. That stop is always in so no one ever uses it. There are two safeguards, but that doesn't mean you can be slack.'

Mum tells me to crawl inside the pipe and keep moving forward. She comes in backwards behind me and twists the valve back into place. The pipe is big enough for me and Mum, but I imagine it would be a tight squeeze for Dad. It slopes so I'm crawling downhill towards a circle of light. The air changes as I get closer to the opening. I breathe deeply and relish the freshness. Mum tells me to wait and squeezes past me. I can see that the pipe comes out at the bottom of the dam. A thick clump of weeds is growing in the middle of the basin and Mum heads towards it. She indicates for me to follow. She reaches into the weeds, lifts up a hidden trapdoor and ushers me inside. I climb down a wooden ladder. Mum follows and closes the trapdoor behind her. Everything goes pitch black. There's fumbling, a click, then light as Mum pulls out a torch from somewhere and flicks it on.

I listen for Dad but the deafening silence tells me he's not here. My heart drops.

Clinging to the ladder, Mum shines the torch back up towards the trapdoor. She pulls out another torch from a brace then climbs down and passes it to me. I turn it on and shine it over the ceiling. I'm standing in a large concrete room. The ceiling is held up by columns. Inside the room are two large shipping containers which run the length of the dam. Water tanks sit along the concrete walls on stands, just higher than the containers. A large pipe runs diagonally from the lowest point in the room and disappears into the wall. There are also drainage grates on the floor, where water is directed away from the cave space and back out to the channel. Mum walks over to the double doors at the end of one of the containers. She speaks at normal volume now, no longer worried about being heard.

'This is your father's bunker, panic room, safe house . . . whatever you want to call it. It's his pride and joy, even though we hoped we'd never actually need to use it.' Mum pulls back the door and flicks some switches on an electric panel board. The lights in the container turn on one by one. I take a step forward and stare, open-mouthed.

Shiny floorboards run the length of the room, which is divided into three sections. I recognise the furniture — all stuff we once had at home. In front of the doorway is our old red leather sofa and matching armchairs positioned around a large rectangular coffee table. I walk through into the second section where there is a large L-shaped desk, three black office chairs and a huge TV screen mounted on the wall. In the third section there's a kitchen with a sink, cooktop and cupboards that run down the wall opposite the desk area. Then, at the very end of the container, a door opens onto what must be a bathroom.

Mum goes to open the other container and switches on the lights. Inside, an arrangement of shelves, drawers and cupboards run the length of the walls. Mum pulls a black garbage bag from a drawer.

'Undress and put your clothes in here then go take a shower. You'll find clean clothes in the fourth cupboard on the right.'

Mum hands me a small traveller's pack of toilet-ries which includes soap, shampoo, conditioner and deodorant.

She doesn't have to tell me twice to strip out of my wet muddy clothes.

'You'll find clean towels in the bathroom,' she calls as I walk towards it. 'The hot water only takes ten minutes, so it should have started to warm up by now.'

The bathroom floor is covered with the same charcoal-coloured tiles as our bathroom at home. Everything else is white. Behind me, Mum turns on monitoring equipment and the TV screen. She pulls out a keyboard and touches the mouse. The screen comes to life. I stare for a moment, then close the bathroom door.

There's a shower, hand basin and toilet. The water is not as hot as I'd like, but I stay in the shower, washing my hair three times before I'm happy all the mud is gone. The pressure isn't the best either, obviously gravity-fed from the tanks. I come back out a few minutes later in my towel. Mum is on the phone, angrily whispering something I can't quite catch. On the TV screen are multiple images of our driveway, our front gate and our house, all from different angles.

Mum hangs up the phone and stands. 'I'm going to take a quick shower too,' she says, closing the bathroom door behind her.

I stare at the TV screen for a while then go to the other storage container to find some clothes. I walk along to the fourth cupboard on the right and open it. Inside is hanging space and drawers. Six outfits hang; three brown camouflage uniforms and three black uniforms complete with boots, balaclavas and ballistic vests. I've only ever seen these in Dad's gun magazines. I go to touch one then pull my hand away. The thought of actually having to wear it is too much right now. I open the drawers and find neatly folded black T-shirts and some underwear. I pull out clothing in my size and start dressing. I go with a black T-shirt and cargo pants because it doesn't feel as confronting as the camo gear.

I move along the cupboards, looking inside each one. There is more clothing, toiletries and enough food to last the three of us for a month at least. Then I open the doors on the left-hand side.

Whoa.

Guns, ammo, explosives, knives, ropes, drones . . . The list goes on.

I step back and take it in. I've seen it all before, used it all, but I've never seen so much of it in one place. It's like Dad's expecting to go to war. This is all kinds of crazy.

Dad being able to build something like this is no surprise, nor that he'd want to. I mean, this is so him. But the fact that he built a bunker, and one so elaborate, and then kept it secret from me – that bit stabs my heart. I don't keep secrets from him. I think of Jonah. Okay, maybe I do. Sometimes. But dating Jonah for six weeks is nothing on having a secret survival bunker for goodness knows how long it's been here. And I was going to tell him about Jonah today!

This bunker must have been built years ago. If it had been installed recently I'd have seen digging equipment and concrete. The earth would have been disturbed, and . . . would Dad have needed a crane to put these containers down here? And to place the concrete walls? They look like they're pre-made, but there's no way Dad could have done all that while I was at school. It would have taken weeks to build this. He must have started when I was a baby. Dad always told me that this dam was built by the people who owned the property before us. He said it was empty because they had built it without checking the quality of the soil first. It turned out the soil didn't hold water, even though the clay rice bays are just thirty metres away on either side. Now that I think about it, that doesn't seem very likely. What are the odds of having a strip of dirt that doesn't hold water between two patches of clay? I never questioned it. Not once, because I believed what he told me. I had no reason to doubt him.

I feel betrayed and distrusted.

The clothes I'm wearing are in my size, too, so it's not like they built the bunker and then forgot about it like a time capsule. They obviously stock it regularly. It's all too much to process. I don't know what it all means, or what it says about me and my family. Do I even know who they are anymore? If I don't know them, do I really know anyone? Who can I trust?

I take a deep breath. I need to focus on what's important right now. One thing at a time.

The big question: who and why.

Who are these people chasing us? Why do they want us dead?

Goosebumps crawl over my arms and to the back of my neck.

It keeps coming back to my parents. What have they done to make these people want to kill them? What have they done that has driven them into hiding for the past seventeen years?

SIX
JONAH

Jonah's heart thumps as hard as it did when he thought Bear might catch him kissing Beth behind the tree. He shouldn't have run off like that. He should have insisted on going with her to tell Bear together. At least then he'd already know how it went. Anything would be better than sitting here waiting to find out.

The younger students wrap up their lessons and clear out of the gym as parents come to collect them. The instructor grabs his things and leaves after the last child is signed out.

Warra walks out of the change room and heads towards Jonah. The only time Warra looks neat and tidy is when he's in his karate uniform. The loose white fabric hangs perfectly all the way down to his ankles, pressed and stark against his brown skin.

His hair is pulled back and tied into a neat ponytail, allowing his whole face to be seen. His dark eyes shine and his square jawline makes him look strong and determined. Warra sits next to Jonah and hands him a towel. Jonah wipes his forehead and puts it down beside him.

'You look like shit,' Warra says. 'You still haven't heard anything?'

'Not yet. But I guess we'll know soon enough.'

Warra turns to the giant clock on the wall.

'Yep, in three minutes.'

Jonah takes a deep breath, looks up to the roof and lets it go. Then he shuts his eyes and does it again.

'He's not going to kill you tonight,' Warra says. 'Too many witnesses. You'll be right.'

Jonah knows Warra is trying to calm him down. Before their last maths test, Warra said something similar. 'You won't fail today. You'll be right.' What he meant was that they wouldn't get their results back until a week later, so he still might fail, just not today. The thought had calmed Jonah down then, but facing Bear is scarier than flunking a maths test.

Fuck, what was he thinking? Bear will eat his nuts for breakfast.

They should have waited a bit longer. Why did Bear have to know now anyway? Why did he ever have to know?

Jonah grabs his phone from his bag and texts Beth. *How'd it go?*

He presses send.

Beth should have waited until after training. But then tomorrow afternoon there's gun club. Before that's not a good time either. Then there's survival camp in a few weeks. She definitely shouldn't tell him before they go out bush together.

Jonah realises there is never a good time to tell Bear. Warra's right. It's a death wish.

Jonah picks up the towel again to wipe the sweat from his forehead. He checks his phone. No reply. Beth always answers quickly. Maybe he should call her.

The phone goes straight to voicemail.

Fuck!

Questions race through Jonah's head. Why isn't Beth answering? Why hasn't she responded to his messages? Would Bear hurt her?

And now they're late. A sickening feeling settles deep in Jonah's gut. He sits on the bench against the wall with his elbows on his knees and waits. He bites down on the inside of his cheek and his eyes dart towards the door as someone enters.

The gymnasium door swings open. Jonah sits up. It's not Beth. He resumes his position with his elbows on his knees and glances at the clock. They're four minutes late.

Where are they?

Bear is never late.

Never. He hates late. He punishes anyone who turns up late with extra push-ups or sit-ups or burpees.

Something's happened. What if Beth told Bear and he lost it? Jonah's never seen Bear lose it before. He's tough and terrifying, but always in control. But what if?

Jonah closes his eyes and takes another long breath. He's not thinking straight. He pulls out his phone again. No messages. He unlocks his screen and brings up Beth's number. He taps her name with his thumb, holds the phone to his ear and braces himself just in case Bear answers. Voicemail. He ends the call without leaving a message.

Beth always replies to his text messages. Her family have a booster so her phone works when she's at home on the farm. There's phone reception up to fifteen kays out of town, so if she was on her way she would be in range by now. Maybe Bear took her phone. Maybe he smashed it . . .

Jonah looks at the door again, then the clock. Something's wrong. They should definitely be here by now.

'Maybe it's not what you think,' Warra says.

Jonah looks at Warra.

Warra glances towards the door. 'Maybe they got a flat tyre,' he suggests.

Jonah gives him another look. 'Yeah, maybe.' Neither of them believe it.

Jonah sighs and reaches for his bag.

'Where're you going?' Warra asks.

'Home,' Jonah says. Which is no lie. But then, somehow, he knows he's going out there. He'll ride his bike tonight if he has to. It's a long way – what would it take? Two hours? He can ride twenty-five kays an hour. He'd be riding in the dark for part of the way, but at least there are no hills.

All Jonah knows is he's got to get out there. Something is terribly wrong. Jonah can feel it. He has to see if Beth's okay.

SEVEN
BETH

Mum places a mug of peppermint tea on the coffee table in front of me and sits down next to me on the couch. Her blonde hair drips water onto her shoulders, forming wet patches on her shirt. I say nothing. She leans forward, then back, like she isn't sure how to begin.

'Just tell me,' I snap.

She nods. 'Okay, okay. Before you were born, your dad and I worked in law enforcement, back in America. We were involved in an operation that went horribly wrong. People died and because of it we received threats. We had to get out quickly. We're independent now, but essentially you've grown up in witness protection, Beth.'

I half-laugh in disbelief. 'What?' My voice is whisper-thin.

'I know what I'm about to tell you will be hard to believe, but please understand that we love you very much and that we'll make sure you have all the help you need to absorb and process this. We've read every book there is about the psychological damage this could cause. We've studied the different phases of grief you will go through, we've anticipated your initial response, we've looked into how you might feel about yourself, about us, about your life . . . Please believe me when I say we had no choice.'

For a moment I'm speechless.

Psychological damage . . . initial response . . . phases of grief . . .

What is she saying?

Mum gives me a long look then continues. 'The man chasing us is a relative of one of the people who died in the operation. He made threats, hired assassins and said he'd never stop until we paid for what had happened. We know what this man is capable of. If we'd stayed in America we'd all be dead by now. The agency gave us various options of protection but none of them really appealed. I had you. I refused to take any risks. Keeping you safe meant everything to me. So, your father and I decided our only option was to cut all ties and leave.' Mum's eyes glass over and her voice wavers. 'In the end the decision was easy, but carrying it out was anything but. We moved here when you were nine months old.'

I stare at Mum.

'From where?'

'Chicago. That's where you were born. We were offered a few different locations but chose Australia because it was most like America. The agency said we should settle in one of the capital cities, but we'd never been to Australia before so we wanted to see the country before deciding where to settle. We flew up to Brisbane, hired a car and intended to drive down to Sydney, Canberra and Melbourne. After travelling around for a while, we started to consider other options. We decided that we wanted to be able to give you the skills that might one day save your life without it seeming strange. Farm life was perfect for that.'

My chest is squeezing the air out of my lungs. I'm hearing what Mum is telling me, but there's something in the back of my mind that I don't want to face.

'We avoided meeting people, at least until we had our story set in our heads like concrete, and we watched as much Australian TV as possible to help master the accent. Once we touched down on Australian soil we started playing a role that has never really stopped.'

Mum pauses and glances up at me. I can tell she's choosing her words very carefully. She takes a sip of tea and continues.

'When we arrived in Deni we fell in love with the place and thought it might be somewhere we'd like to live permanently. We based ourselves in a neighbouring town for a few weeks while we researched names, sporting clubs, real estate, local industry, jobs we might be able to do —'

'Stop!' I say. Names? It's too much at once. I can't listen to what Mum's saying because my mind is still stuck back at Chicago. 'What is . . . I can't . . . I'm . . .' My mouth is so dry I can't swallow.

'Drink some tea,' Mum says.

I bring the mug to my lips and take the tiniest mouthful. I'm struggling to get my head around this. I look at Mum. She is leaning forward again. There's a worry line between her eyebrows. She looks like my mum, like the person who raised me, but who is she really? Who am I?

The last thought comes as a punch.

Miller . . . My surname skitters around my mind, bounces off the inside of my skull.

It's the town's generational name. Half the town are Millers, but we're the only family not related to any of the others. What did Mum say about researching names?

An awful feeling creeps into my stomach.

My name . . .

I am Elizabeth Miller, aren't I? Elizabeth Miller, only child of Gregory and Lucy, with no grand-parents, aunts, uncles or cousins. Elizabeth Miller who loves hanging out with friends. House captain, karate black belt, trap shooting champion. Jonah's girlfriend. Farm kid. Member of the local netball, tennis, gun club, karate club and motocross teams. I go to Deni High School. I am and have always been Elizabeth Miller.

But what if she never existed?

I look at Mum. 'What's my name?'

'Kennedy. Kennedy Jane. Jane is your surname.'

The name rolls around inside my head, foreign and intrusive. I push it away and my thoughts turn to something more pressing than my name.

'So this guy has Dad? What's he going to do to him?' I ask.

Mum's eyes drop. 'I don't know. I've called for an extraction team.' Mum sees me frown. 'Specially trained police will come and get us out. Dad too, hopefully, but it will take some time because of where we are.'

'Hopefully?'

Mum hesitates. 'The man after us, Carlos, went to jail. His hatred has had a long time to fester. His sixteen-year-old son was killed during the oper- ation and Carlos blamed your dad for his death. Presumably, that's still the case.'

'But they'll get Dad out, won't they? They'll find whoever took him?'

Mum purses her lips. 'I don't know, Beth. I don't know what will happen. All I know is we're safe here. No one knows where we are. Carlos won't find us. I haven't even disclosed our exact location to the extraction team yet.'

'When will they get here?'

'I don't know. We've been on our own for a long time. We're not in their data bank. They're doing some checks on their end and calling us back.'

'But Dad needs them now. What if they don't arrive in time? We have to get him out.'

'No. Now that you're here you're not going anywhere until the threat is over. The extraction team will get us out, then we'll contact our guys back in Chicago to help relocate us.'

'What do you mean?' I ask.

'We may have to move again.'

'No, no, no, no.' I shake my head. 'I don't want to move. My friends, my school . . . I want to stay here.'

'We'll talk about this later. When this is all over.'

'But the police will arrest Carlos, right?'

'Even with Carlos back in jail, we might still be in danger. Now that our location is compromised his hired assassins might keep coming after us. It's too early to make these decisions now, but if the time comes we'll do what we have to do. Even if that means cutting all ties, changing our names, and moving again so we can't be found.'

I laugh, nervous hysteria rising in my chest and closing my throat. 'There's no way I'm doing that. No way.'

'They will kill us, Beth.'

'Then we'll kill them first.'

Mum frowns. I know how ridiculous I sound. But I don't *want* to cut ties and start my life over.

It's my life. Deni is all I've ever known. Outrage churns inside me. The last seventeen years are my entire childhood. No one is going to take that from me without a fight.

Mum looks away. She stands, goes to a cupboard at the far side of the desk and pulls out a large map of our property. She lays it on the coffee table then places a clear plastic sheet that shows the channel systems and pipelines over the top.

'We looked at different locations all over the world for the best place to hide and make a new life. Deni was perfect. This farm was perfect. The channel system connects every part of the property and provides us with cover if we need to escape. Farm life allowed us to raise you to be able to shoot and drive at a young age without it seeming strange, and we've taught you how to fight and survive out here. We chose the town's most popular name so it would be harder for them to find us. We thought of everything. We've prepared you for this day, to give you the very best chance of survival.'

I rock back against my seat and try to digest what Mum is telling me. It feels like she just fed me poison. Every cell in my body is revolted by it, rejecting and repelling her words.

Who am I? And what happens now?

Does knowing my real name change who I am? Am I still the same Beth Miller?

Mum sits up, staring at the TV screen.

A white van turns into our driveway and slowly makes its way towards the house. I gasp and move so I can get a better look at the screen. The van pulls up outside our front door. The driver and passenger doors of the van open and two men get out. They're wearing balaclavas. The back door slides open and a third man jumps down and steps into view. He throws the other men M16 assault rifles, keeping one for himself, and then slams the door shut.

There's no sign of Dad, but that doesn't mean he's not inside the van.

The men move straight to our front door, then two of them step back to give the first man more room. He brings the rifle up to the lock and fires.

I flinch and my hands fly up to cover my mouth.

The men step straight inside our house without hesitation, like they know we're not home, and close the door behind them.

EIGHT
JONAH

Jonah places one arm through the handle of his bag, shrugs it onto his back and starts jogging for home. Then he stops. Beth lives on the opposite side of town. It's a six-kay run to Jonah's, then that plus another fifty kays out to Beth's place on his bike. He needs a plan, someone with a car.

Jonah hears it before he sees it. A familiar throaty grumble, idling at the intersection. He can't help but turn towards it. It's Trent Granger's Holden Maloo. All black, tinted windows and black rims, lowered right down with a bit of negative camber and Toyo tyres. If it wasn't Trent's he'd admire it, but the guy's a wanker. Jonah's surprised he's got the balls to still drive it in town after what happened. It's not exactly inconspicuous. The ute keeps to the left and edges along, close to the pavement until it's beside him. The passenger window glides down.

'Hey, dude,' Trent says.

'Trent.' Jonah is short with him. He knows what he wants. 'No point hanging around in town for Carly. Mum's picking her up.' Jonah knows he sounds like a snotty little brother, but he doesn't care. He doesn't want Carly hanging around a drug-fucked loser like Trent.

Trent holds his hands up, palms facing out. 'Hey, I'm not here for Carly. I just stopped to say hi. I'm heading home from the gym. Carly said she's got homework anyway.'

Jonah frowns through the window and takes a better look at him. There's a gym bag on the passenger seat and Trent's hair is wet like he just showered. All the scabs he had on his face have healed and his eyes look clear. Focused. Is this the same guy who smashed up the front door of the hospital?

'What are you doing anyway? Carly said you had training tonight.'

'Bear didn't show. So, you're staying out at your parents?'

'Yeah. They think it's best I stay out of town for a while. And Dad's working up north for another month, so it's good for Mum to have someone staying out there with her.'

'Can I get a lift out there with you?'

'To my place?'

'To Bear's.'

'You've gotta be fucking kidding.'

'You can drop me at your gate. I'll walk the rest of the way.'

'Mate, we're ten kays short of their place. And the answer is no. No fucking way.'

'Please, Trent. I won't tell my parents you took me. If they find out I went, I'll say I hitchhiked. Please, it could be a matter of life and death.'

'Yeah, mine.'

'No, Beth's . . .'

Trent looks at Jonah. 'Why? Man, don't tell me you're shaggin' Bear's kid.'

'Don't talk about her like that.'

Trent stares at Jonah then shakes his head.

'Jesus, dude, you must have rocks in your head. Her old man's hardcore. You heard about my run-in with him, right? He caught me out the back of the gym one night after training and went ape-shit. Thought I was dealing. He lifted me off the ground with one hand like it was nothing. Told me if I ever gave drugs to any of his students he'd kick my arse into next week. I believed him too. The way he looked at me. It was like he wanted to pulverise my face right then and there.'

'I won't tell Bear you drove me out. I'll stick to the same story: I hitchhiked.'

Trent stares at me and sighs.

'I'm not taking you all the way. How will you make the last ten kays?'

Jonah's hopes lift. Trent's going to do it. Jonah wishes he had his bike, he could easily ride the last ten kays. He turns and looks back at the gymnasium. Warra's bike is still sitting by the entrance. It's the only way Warra gets around, but maybe he'd let him borrow it for a couple of hours.

'Can you wait here for a sec?'

Trent sighs.

'Wait one sec,' Jonah says. 'Please . . .' He backs away, keeping his eye on Trent like that will somehow make him stay put until he returns. 'Don't go anywhere.'

Jonah runs inside. Warra is still sitting where he left him.

'Hey, Warra,' Jonah says.

'What's going on?'

'Something's not right, man. I'm going out there. I wondered if I could borrow your bike?'

'You riding all that way now?'

'No, I'm getting a lift out there, but I might have to ride back. It's only fifty kays. I'll be a couple of hours max.' Jonah tilts his head to the side as Warra smiles. 'I can do it, easy. Your bike's got lights, hasn't it?'

'Of course. What time will you be back?'

'Don't know. Depends how long I'm out there.'

'Just bring it to school in the morning.'

'You sure?'

'Yeah, man. Do what you gotta do. I've got my legs. I'll use them to get home.' Warra smiles again.

'Thanks, man. I owe you.'

They bump fists.

'Good luck, dude. I'll send the cops out if you don't come back,' Warra says.

Jonah laughs. When he's back outside he sends a message to his mum.

Heading over to Warra's after training to help with an assignment. Might work late so don't wait up. I'll ride his bike home later.

Jonah hates lying to his mum, but she'd never let him go out to Beth's place this late. Jonah can deal with the consequences tomorrow. Right now the most important thing is making sure Beth is okay.

Jonah grabs Warra's bike and helmet, throws his gym bag over his shoulder and makes a dash for Trent's car. When Trent sees him coming he opens the hard lid of the ute. There's nothing in the tray, not even dust. It's pristine.

'That bike had better not scratch the duco,' Trent says. He takes off his jacket and lays it on the floor of the tray. They carefully lift Warra's bike into the back, onto the jacket, and Trent closes the lid.

Trent doesn't talk much on the way out. Jonah feels guilty for being short with him earlier. It's obvious Trent's clean, at least for now. Maybe he really is trying, maybe he'll stay clean this time. Deni never forgets though. Jonah can't see how he'll get his job back, or that anyone else in town will employ him. It's gutsy to return.

'I really appreciate you driving me,' Jonah says.

There's a look in Trent's eye that makes Jonah feel sorry for him.

'Yeah, well, I can see it backfiring. So just don't drop me in it, okay?'

'Don't worry, I won't. I'll say I hitched with a stranger passing through town. It's all my doing anyway. It's not like you tried to convince me to go. I convinced you to take me.'

'Yeah, but I'll be the bad guy no matter what. When you screw up in this town, you're always going to be the screw-up. And once you're the town screw-up, you get the blame for everything.'

'Then why come back?' Jonah realises his question sounds aggressive. 'I mean, wouldn't it be easier to start over somewhere new?'

'I came back to make things right . . . for my parents more than anything else. I owe them that. I found out Mum stopped going into town after I left. Couldn't stand the gossip, the shame. I feel shit about that. What I did wasn't her fault. Mum's a good person, and she's done a lot for Deni. If it was just me, I'd tell the whole town to go screw them-selves. But, here I am, back home and sucking up to those fuckers for her.'

Jonah hasn't thought about Trent's mum since Trent was arrested. He can't even remember when he saw her last. Before the night Trent lost it, Carol Granger was on every committee in town, all over every charity. She even raised money for the hospital Trent smashed up. But in a small town tongues start wagging. People judge. Suddenly it was her fault that Trent was such a mess.

Jonah even heard his own mum saying venomous things, but she had a right to because Carly was involved. Jonah was there when Ida told Carol to keep her son away from her daughter. She confronted her in the main street, made a real scene. At the time it seemed reasonable because Carly was so much younger and Trent was a bad influence. Ida was being a good mother and Jonah was on her side because he didn't want Carly anywhere near Trent either. He stood by his mum, his chest puffed out like a rooster, while Ida gave Carol a serve, like they had a special right to do that. He flinches at the memory now.

'It's big of you.' Jonah stops because his tone isn't right and somehow his words sound sarcastic. 'I mean it,' he says. 'It would have been hard to come back after what happened. I . . . I admire you for that.'

Trent sucks in air like he's about to cry.

'Thanks, man,' he says. 'That means a lot.'

This is suddenly too weird and Jonah is relieved when they reach the gate and get out of the car.

They lift the bike out of the tray, then Jonah puts his hand out to shake Trent's. 'Good luck, mate,' he says.

'I think you're the one who's going to need the luck,' Trent says with a laugh as he closes the lid of his ute.

Jonah waits for Trent to drive away before he starts the ten-kay ride to Beth's. He tucks the legs of his karate pants into his socks and starts pedalling. Warra's bike is good on the dirt. Ten kays isn't going to take long. Suddenly, Jonah doesn't know how to prepare himself for what might happen when he gets there. Why couldn't Bear make training? Why couldn't Beth answer his calls? Surely Bear wouldn't hurt Beth? Maybe Jonah should've told the police and had them come with him. He pulls out his phone and checks the signal, even though he knows he's too far out of town for reception. He should have called some of his school mates earlier. Audrey's mum's a cop. Jonah could have told her his concerns. Or Carly's best friend, Lana. Her dad's a sergeant and really nice. Jonah probably could have convinced him to drive out to check on Beth.

The lower the sun sinks towards the horizon, the quicker the air temperature drops. The wind bites at Jonah's face. He drops his head and cycles harder. He wriggles his fingers, already stiff from the cold, then takes one hand off the handlebars and tucks it into the pocket of his jacket. His karate pants are thin and the cool air cuts straight through them. He should have changed. He should have thought things through more instead of heading straight out into what could be anything. Jonah knows his imagination is getting the better of him, but he can't stop the thoughts. What if Bear lost his temper and hurt Beth? What if it's a murder scene? What would he do then? Jonah pulls himself out of his own head. As if. That's ridiculous. There'll be a perfectly reasonable explanation for everything. He checks his phone again, but, of course, there is still no signal.

In the case that nothing is wrong and there is a perfectly good reason why they didn't make training, Jonah tries to think up his own explanation as to why he just rushed all the way out here to check on Beth. He doesn't want to look stupid for jumping to conclusions, but nothing realistic comes to mind. Nothing that sounds truthful anyway. He's just going to have to say he got worried when they didn't show up, so he came out to check that Beth was okay. Who knows, Bear might even think it shows how much he cares and see Jonah as thoughtful and courageous, someone who would look after Beth. It could impress him. Although Bear and Jonah both know that Beth doesn't need looking after. She's smart, fit, and further advanced in karate than Jonah. She can whip him in a fight whenever she wants. Understandable really, considering who her dad is.

Jonah pushes away his angst and rides on. Being laughed at is a far better outcome than finding something terrible has happened. He can handle being laughed at.

Jonah pedals harder to increase his pace. Only a couple of kays to go.

NINE
BETH

Mum and I stare at the screen, our mouths hanging open.

'Where's Dad? What have they done to him? We have to go and find him,' I say.

'That's out of the question,' Mum replies. Her voice is steady. 'Your father and I agreed on this. Our plan was to get you to safety and stay put, no matter what. You didn't ask to be born into this, so it's our job to make sure you're safe.'

'Would they have already killed him?'

'I don't know.'

'Are you sure they're going to?'

'I don't know, Beth. A lot of time has passed since Carlos was arrested.'

'Well, until we know, we have to try,' I say.

'We're not leaving this bunker. Your father and I made a pact. He made me promise.'

'My life isn't more valuable than his,' I plead.

'Yes, it is,' Mum replies firmly.

'How can you say that?'

'Because I'm your mother. And it's the natural way of things.'

'But he's *my* father!'

'Beth . . .' She says it like it's the end of the conversation, but then her eyes look away, like there's more she's not saying.

'What?'

'Nothing.'

'Tell me what it is. You're hiding something.'

Mum frowns at the screen. 'What the . . .?' Her pupils expand and she grabs my arm. 'Who's that?'

I turn slowly, following her gaze to the TV screen, bracing myself for what I might see. Someone on a bike is turning into our driveway. Someone wearing white karate pants.

My blood turns stone cold.

'Jonah,' I whisper.

'Jonah Keath?' asks Mum.

'Yes. He's my . . . We're . . . my boyfriend.'

'What?'

'I was going to tell you today, I swear. Then Dad didn't show up to training.'

'Oh no,' Mum says. She groans.

My breath catches in my throat as I think about those men shooting our door, barging into our house. Aggressive and ruthless.

'We have to stop him.' Mum grabs the phone. 'Sometimes I get signal in our driveway. Beth, what's his number? Quick.'

Panic seizes my brain. 'Er . . . It's in my phone.' I try to remember, but I've never actually looked at his number. I stand motionless – clutching my hands together, staring at the screen – as Jonah rides down our driveway towards our house, towards three men with M16s. My face crumples and tears flush my eyes.

'We have to stop him,' I say to Mum.

'We won't make it in time,' she whispers. 'He's about come into view from the house.'

Jonah cycles around the bend and enters the straight, the last two hundred metres of our driveway.

He's seconds away from the house.

Mum and I are frozen. We stand, hearts in our throats, hands over our mouths. Uselessly watching, hopelessly waiting . . .

TEN
JONAH

Jonah slows down when he rounds the corner and cycles up the final stretch of driveway. It feels good to be rid of some of that nervous energy. Jonah's never done anything like this before. He's never had to. He feels gallant and strong, going all out for love. If Bear is violent, he will stand up to defend Beth, even though he knows he'd never win a fight against him. If he's not violent, they will talk, man-to-man. He will tell Bear he loves Beth, that he'll treat her right and that he can be trusted. It's what Trent should have done when he started seeing Carly. Jonah's parents never liked him. The drugs were the kicker, but even before things got really bad Trent never tried to make it any better. He never made an effort to win Ida over, probably knew it was a lost cause. Jonah's learned from Trent's mistake.

He won't slink around behind Lucy's and Bear's backs like that. He wouldn't dare. God, Bear could snap him like a twig. That man's a giant. A machine.

It's still light out but the house is dark and quiet, like no one is home. The van Jonah saw on the street earlier that afternoon is parked alongside the house. Do they have visitors? Is that all this is? Could Bear really be like everyone else and have pulled a sickie because he had more fun things to do? This could be so embarrassing. Jonah hesitates for a moment. Maybe he should turn around and go. But what if they've already seen him? They'll laugh at him. Jonah's face burns. This is going to be so humiliating.

Jonah rides up to the side of the house and onto the concrete. He gets off the bike and leans it against the wall, trying to make enough noise for them to hear him. Jonah tries to act casual, like he visits people fifty kays out of town on a whim all the time. He takes off Warra's helmet and hangs it on the handlebars, never taking his eye off the front door. Something doesn't look right. He looks more closely and realises the front door is damaged. His stomach drops. Are they bullet holes? Jesus. Did Bear do that? Jonah backs away, glancing at his bike. He wants to run but he can't leave without finding out if Beth's okay. Jonah's heart thumps in his chest like a battle drum. He fights the urge to get out of there.

The front door swings back. Jonah's startled. He jumps, then stumbles backwards in fright as a man wearing a balaclava barrels towards him. Bear? Jonah tries to say the word but nothing comes out. It's not Bear. This guy is much smaller. A semi-automatic assault rifle levels with his face. Jonah freezes.

'Inside,' the man says.

'Bear . . .' Jonah knows it's not Bear, but it's all he can think to say.

The man cracks the butt of the gun above Jonah's eye. Pain spears through him as the flesh splits. He goes down and thuds hard onto the concrete.

In a flash the man is on top of him, his knee pressed firmly into Jonah's back. He grabs Jonah's wrists and zip-ties them together. Jonah is then thrust into darkness as a hood goes over his head.

He's dragged inside. Jonah can hear two other men talking. Then the front door is slammed shut.

Jonah breathes fast and hard – heart hammering, panic rising.

What the fuck is going on?

ELEVEN
BETH

A scream rises from somewhere deep inside me. Mum holds me, trying to calm me down, but I shake her off. Tears streak down my face.

'No! Jonah! Mum, we've got to do something.'

Mum places her hands on my shoulders and moves right in front of my face.

'Okay, okay, okay . . . Calm down. Beth, we have to stay calm. We are no help to Jonah while we're hysterical.'

'They're going to kill him!' Fresh tears come and I wipe them away before they fall off my cheeks. 'Oh my God, what's happening? Who are those men? They smashed Jonah's face.'

Mum lets me go and leans on the desk, like she's taking a moment for herself. She slams her fist down so hard I jump. She can't lose it now. I need her to be calm. I need her to know what to do.

'Okay,' she says. She closes her eyes. 'Okay,' she says again to herself. 'This is not good. This is not going to plan. What the hell is he doing out here anyway?'

'I don't know. He knew I was going to tell Dad about us. I guess he got worried when we didn't turn up to training.' I stop and try to control my breathing. 'What do we do?'

'*We* do nothing. You're not leaving this bunker. I'll go and get Jonah.'

'I'm not staying here by myself.'

'Yes, you are.'

'No. You can't do it on your own. What if they capture you as well? Our chances are better if we both go.'

'I'm not arguing about this, Beth.'

I follow Mum to the storage container. She puts on a ballistic vest. I grab one too and do the same.

'Beth!'

'I'm going with you,' I say, my temper rising. 'I'm going no matter what you say. If you go without me, I'll follow you. If you stay here, I'll go on my own.'

Mum stops. I hold her gaze. She takes in a sharp breath.

'Now is not the time for this, Elizabeth.'

I stare at Mum in disbelief. I've run through freezing slush to avoid capture, I've been told I'm not Elizabeth, and now I'm being holed up in this bunker when my boyfriend's life is in danger. Those creeps who have my dad, who are hunting us, just smashed Jonah's face with a rifle and now Mum's chastising me? Is she even who she says she is? Is she my mother? I don't doubt who my father is, I'm definitely from his gene pool. But Mum is short and petite with pale skin and thin lips. We look nothing alike. What if . . .?

'I'm going!' I cry. 'Now is exactly the time. You *lied* to me. For my whole life, you've lied. I don't even know who I am! Or who you are. Are you even my real mum? You don't get to tell me what to do.'

Mum's hand cracks across my face. A stinging, silencing slap.

Tears flood my eyes.

'I'm sorry,' I stammer. I'm shocked at what I said. I'm ashamed by how much I wanted to hurt her.

'I'm sorry too.' Mum's voice is calm, controlled and gentle. 'Beth, you've just had a terrible shock and I know it's a lot to take in. But right now you need to hold it together. I need you to hold it together. For us and for Jonah. Can you do that?'

My chest heaves, sobs rising in my throat.

'I am your real mum, Beth. I'm the same person you've always known. That hasn't changed. We're still the same people and I'll do whatever it takes to protect you *and* Jonah. You may doubt a lot of things in the coming weeks, but you don't have to doubt me. Okay?'

I nod. 'I'm still going,' I say stubbornly.

Mum exhales and runs both hands through her hair. 'Beth, I need you to stay here.'

'It's not happening.'

She nods. Looks away from me.

'You are so much like your father.' She smiles sadly as she says it. 'This is all against the plan . . .' After another moment she continues. 'Okay, we do this together. But, by God, you had better do *exactly* what I say, when I say it. Do you understand?'

'I will,' I say. 'Exactly what you say.'

'When I say it.' Mum throws me a black jacket. 'Put that on over your vest.' She opens the gun cupboard, chooses a firearm for both of us and puts a few sticks of gelignite in a pouch on her belt. She goes to shut the cupboard door then stops. She stares at the drones, then lifts one out of its box.

'I'll cause a diversion and lure them outside.' Mum hands me an earpiece. 'We've seen three men, but there could be more. Only go in when I have confirmed their numbers and the house is clear. You got that? I'll keep them occupied while you get Jonah out.'

'Yes,' I say, holding my voice steady. Seeing Jonah get thrown to the ground by that man gave me a huge rush of adrenaline and now my hands are trembling. Mum notices and wraps hers around mine.

'Are you sure you can do this? You have to hold it together out there, no matter what happens.

You do what it takes to survive. You make hard decisions.' Mum pauses. 'I know you're ready for this, Beth.'

I nod because I don't want her to hear the fear in my voice.

'We'll travel down the channel towards the house. When we reach the pump shed we'll separate. I'll go to the front of the house, you go round the back. You know how to get in. I'll create a diversion out the front, long enough for you to get inside, get Jonah and get out. I'll do what I can to cover you. Then we meet back here. Do *not* wait for me. When I tell you to go, you go. I'll see to it that you have enough time to reach the bunker. And if I say we have to abort the mission, we abort immediately, no questions asked. Understand?'

There is a fierce determination to Mum's orders and I'm not sure if she realises it, but a slight American accent has crept into her speech.

'Beth, do you understand everything I just said?'

'Yes,' I whisper.

'Are you ready?' Mum hands me a magazine full of ammo and another for the pouch on my belt. 'You're going to be fine. We've trained you for this.' She hands me a headset and a knife in a canvas holster. She bends down to strap her knife to her ankle. I copy.

'Yes,' I say. 'I'm ready.'

'Good. Now let's go and rescue your boyfriend.' Mum winks as she says it.

A smile curls on my lips. She's still my mum.

We leave the bunker the same way we entered, securing the stop in the pipe behind us.

'If they're chasing you, lead them away from here,' Mum instructs. 'You know this farm better than they do. Use that against them. The location of the bunker must never be revealed. It's your safe haven, your ticket to survival. The extraction team will be getting ready for despatch so help will be on the way soon. If I'm not back yet and the phone rings, answer it. Only disclose the exact location of the bunker if they are in position to extract you there and then. Do *not* disclose your location under any other circumstances. Do you understand?'

'Yes.' I listen hard, even though I know it's not going to come down to me being in the bunker on my own. I won't let that happen.

'Once you get Jonah back to the bunker, he must not leave until the police arrive. If we pull this off and rescue him, he's with us until the end.'

'Got it,' I say. It's the only part of this plan I like.

'And Beth . . .' I look at Mum because her tone has softened. 'If you make it back and I don't, you must promise me that you won't come looking for me. You make decisions with your head, not your heart. It's hard and it's cold, but sometimes it's the only way to survive.'

I look away. The brutality of the situation hits me. I don't know if I can think hard and cold.

Mum's totally focused, in combat mode. She moves light and fast, pulling a balaclava down over her face. I copy her every move.

When we emerge from the bunker the sun is sinking low in the sky. We use the channel for cover as far as we can, then crawl the rest of the way to the house dam, which is full of water. We lie flat against the outside bank so we can't be seen from the house. The house is quiet and the van is parked alongside it. That's the side where Mum will cause a diversion.

'Check the van too,' I say. 'In case Dad's in there.'

Mum nods and indicates for me to stay quiet. She uses hand signals to communicate, the same signals Dad teaches at survival camp.

'You ready?' she whispers. Her voice comes through the earpiece.

I nod. I know what to do. I have shrubs to my right to use as cover until Mum gives the all clear. Then I'll sprint the last little bit to reach the back of the house.

I watch Mum place the drone down on the ground and start it up. She takes it straight up as fast as it can travel. Twenty metres, fifty metres, eighty metres, then it disappears and can't be heard. Once it reaches its maximum height, Mum straps the screen to her wrist so she doesn't lose visual and starts moving forward. My stomach lurches to see her go. My anger towards her has completely vanished. She sacrificed her life – everyone and everything she loved – for me and now she's risking it all again for Jonah.

Mum runs to the van. She checks inside, then moves to the side of the house. She doubles back around to avoid going past the glass doors, then she moves out of sight.

All is quiet and I wait. My palms start to sweat, like they do before a fight. My stomach churns. What if I can't do it? What if I freeze up? Or worse, what if we're already too late?

'Get ready.' Mum's voice comes through the headset loud and clear. 'There's going to be a bang. It's just a tree exploding.'

Mum comes into view out the front of the house. She climbs up a tree, then springs down and sprints out of sight.

The bang is like distant fireworks, not as loud as I expected. A large limb of the tree falls to the ground with a sickening crack.

Three men come into view, guns in the air. There's yelling at first, confusion. They look around as they make their way towards the tree.

'Beth, go!'

I sprint to the corner of the house and I'm around the back in seconds. I enter through the enclosed veranda, then the laundry door. I tread lightly, just in case they can hear me on the wooden floorboards from outside. I'm in the lounge area when I see Jonah lying face down with his head covered in black fabric. His hands and feet are zip-tied together. I peek outside through the glass door before crouching down beside Jonah.

'Jonah, it's Beth,' I whisper in his ear. He lies as still as stone. For a terrible moment I think he's unconscious, but then he nods. I work fast, removing his hood first. He squints as I take it off. Blood is smeared down one side of his face. I pull the knife from my ankle and cut free his wrists and ankles.

'Beth, get out. Get out now!' Mum's words are laced with angst.

'Are you hurt? Can you run?' I ask Jonah.

'I'm okay,' he says.

'C'mon then, hurry!'

We waste no time. Jonah follows me back out to the laundry and I hesitate. I can't see or hear any of the men. Is it safe to go? I pull my rifle around to the front so I can access it if needed.

'Beth. Get out now. Go!'

There's gunfire out the front and then I hear heavy footsteps running through the house as we fly from the veranda.

'One's coming around the back. Go left,' Mum commands.

'The karate kid's gone!' someone yells.

'You were supposed to stay with him,' another voice answers.

We make it to the gate that leads to another dam on the other side of the house and use the trees as cover.

Jonah stays close. We sprint towards our machinery shed. There's a motorbike in there. If I make it to the shed, I know I'll get away. I can go anywhere on this farm on that bike, and if I use the channels and banks there's no way they can follow me in the van.

'Keep going, Beth,' Mum's voice urges in my ear. 'Use the channels to make your way back to the bunker.'

There's gunfire. I stop running and turn around, my heart racing. Where is she?

'Don't stop, Beth.' Mum's voice is clear through the headset.

I exhale. She's still alive. I may not be able to see her, but she can see us via the drone.

We are one hundred metres from the house. Safe enough, but on the wrong side.

'They've spotted you, Beth. Go, run! I'll cover you.'

I pick up speed and sprint hard towards the shed, arms and legs pumping fast. I feel as light as the wind. There's more gunfire, but I hear Jonah close behind me so I don't stop.

'The motorbike,' I say.

We race around the back of the shed and pull open the side door. We're inside, hidden from view.

I reach the bike. Like all our farm vehicles, the key is in the ignition. It kick-starts first go.

'Get on,' I yell to Jonah. I rev it high so it won't stall and we burn out into the clearing. I know where to go, where they can't follow, but I hesitate. I need to make sure Mum is safe too. I need to distract them so she can get away. Instead of turning right, I turn left, back towards the house. I see Mum pressed against the far corner of the house. Two men wearing black balaclavas are running from the trees into the clearing. They're carrying guns. The third, also wearing a bala-clava, is standing on the lawn with his back to Mum.

'No, Beth! Go back.'

As she says it she steps out and the man on the lawn turns from me to her. He raises his gun and points it at her chest. It's close range.

'Mum, look out!' I scream.

A flash comes from the man's gun. One, two, three rounds fire. Mum's body shunts backwards with the force of the missiles. Her arms fly out to the sides as she hits the ground.

The world spins in slow motion. The air is sucked from my lungs like I'm in a vacuum. Everything I see and hear is distorted.

She's hit.

Mum's hit.

Her body is motionless. The man stands over her. He bends down and pulls back her balaclava.

'It's the mother,' he yells to his friends. His words are picked up by Mum's microphone and come through my earpiece. He unbuckles the drone's screen from Mum's wrist then indicates to the others. They look up as he lowers the drone. In a few seconds it's in view. The two men stand watching it as it lowers. When it's close enough one of them raises his rifle and pulls the trigger, blowing it to bits. The other guy cracks up laughing and fires a few shots into the sky out of excitement, then he howls like a wolf at the moon.

'What did you do that for? Idiots! We could have used that,' says the man who shot Mum.

My bike idles beneath me. Jonah and I are frozen to the spot. The man leans down and pulls the headpiece off Mum's ear. He looks up, directly at me. His eyes and lips stand out against the black mask. A chill passes through me as our gaze locks across the distance.

'Well, aren't you something else.' He laughs. 'You're the one we're really after. You may as well come in now.'

I'm stunned, transfixed.

'Beth . . .' Jonah's voice floats into my head and swirls around for a moment before I can register it.

I pull off my headpiece and hold it away from me. I twirl it so he can see, then throw it onto the ground. I rev the bike a few times.

'Hold on,' I say to Jonah.

The men point their guns in our direction. I plant my foot firmly on the ground and give the bike everything. The back wheel spins as the bike turns a one-eighty and with the rattle of gunfire behind us, we burn away.

Jonah holds on tight, always leaning the right way. We've both done motocross and know how to ride. We go through channels, paddocks and trees and I pull up just short of the main channel, as close to the bunker as possible without giving away its location. Jonah gets off the bike, staggers away from me and vomits.

'Help me lift the bike down to the cumbungi,' I say. 'We have to hide it without leaving tracks.'

Jonah helps me without saying a word.

'We have a safe place to go to,' I say. 'We can call for help from there.'

'Beth . . .' Jonah says, blood oozing from a cut above his eye.

I turn and walk towards the feeder channel.

'Beth, are you okay?'

I keep walking. I can't talk right now. I can't think. If I do I will fall apart.

'We just need to get to the bunker,' I say.

Jonah follows.

'We need to call the cops,' he says.

'Mum said specially trained police were on the way. We can't call the local guys. I have to do what she said.'

'Beth, your mum was just shot. I don't think those rules apply anymore.'

'But if I'd just done what she said, she wouldn't have been shot. I was supposed to make hard decisions, to think with my head, but I didn't. If I hadn't turned around . . .' I trail off, too afraid to finish my sentence. 'She said not to call the police. Those guys will kill them. I don't want their blood on my hands too.'

'All police are trained, Beth,' Jonah says.

'We're not calling them. We're talking about people we know, Jonah. Our friends' parents.'

'Yeah, and we're talking about your parents, Beth. And us. When I was in the house those men said they were going to make your dad watch you die. Who the hell are these guys and why do they want to kill you?'

I stop walking and stare at Jonah.

'They said that? They want Dad to watch me *die*?'

'Yes. Who are they?'

'I don't know. They've been hired by someone called Carlos. Mum and Dad used to be secret agents, or police or something. I don't know. It was years ago, in America, before I was born. Something bad happened and people got hurt. This Carlos guy must still blame Dad for his son dying and now he wants Dad to suffer the same fate. That's why he wants me. But, that must mean . . . Dad's alive.'

I feel a tiny flicker of hope at this realisation.

Jonah's staring at me, his mouth open.

'We moved here under witness protection,' I blurt out. Then I stop, my shoulders slacken and my arms hang by my sides. 'Can you believe that?'

Jonah just gapes at me.

'Of course you can't believe it. I can't either. I only found out today. I'm not Elizabeth Miller. My real name is Kennedy Jane.'

I turn away and start walking back towards the pipe. I don't want to see that doubt enter his eyes. That question of who I am. The realisation that I am not who he thought I was.

'It's a shock, hey,' I say. Tears sting my eyes. I blink and breathe them away. 'Talk about pulling the rug out from under me.' I leave it at that. I need the numbness in my chest, the deadness in my mind. Think hard, think cold. If I don't they will kill us all.

Jonah runs to catch up.

'Beth, there's something . . . I need to . . .'

'Jonah, we're not safe yet and I need to think. Let's just get to the bunker and work out how we're going to rescue Mum.'

'Beth, she was shot. At close range.'

'She was wearing a ballistic vest.' I unzip my jacket and show him mine.

Again Jonah is speechless. I can see he's confused, that he wants to scream 'Who are you people?'. I know he must, because that question is on repeat inside my head right now. I walk over to him and kiss him hard on the lips. I go to pull away, but he grabs me, holds me and kisses me back.

'Jonah,' I say. 'I need to know . . .'

He gently brushes my cheek with his thumb.

'I'm with you all the way,' he says. 'Regardless of what your name is.' The power of his words risks giving me a total meltdown. 'But I've got to tell you something.'

'Wait,' I say, 'I need to stay tough and clear-headed. Please don't tell me anything that will interfere with that right now. If we want to survive, we have to remain focused.'

Our eyes connect. His breathing is rapid, like he's in pain, but whatever he's got to tell me will have to wait.

He nods. 'Okay.'

We walk along the muddy channel in silence then crawl the rest of the way to the pipe that takes us into the dry dam. Jonah enters first. I close the valve then follow him into the basin and open the trapdoor.

Again, Jonah goes first and I shut the trap behind us. I climb down the ladder, dropping the last couple of steps onto the concrete floor before heading straight into the operational container. I snatch up the phone and press redial.

TWELVE
JONAH

Jonah stares around the bunker while he follows Beth. Everything about Bear makes sense now. His discipline, his drive, his protectiveness of Beth. Jonah checks out the shipping containers and equipment. To think that all this time, everyone in the town has been trained in karate, firearms and survival skills by a secret agent. It's like he's trained his own army.

Jonah stands in the middle of the lounge area and watches Beth pick up the phone.

'Um . . .' she stammers. 'I'm calling on behalf of Lucy Miller. She called this number earlier. We're in witness protection. Can I speak to someone about that?'

Beth stands even though there is a chair right next to her. 'I don't know. It was seventeen years ago . . . But Mum was shot, just now, by the men after us,' she says. Her voice wavers. Jonah wonders how she'll be when all this sinks in.

'I don't know if the program still covers us. I've only just found out. No, he's missing. I think they have him too, but I'm not sure . . . I saw three, but there could be more . . . I don't know. No, we haven't called the police. My witness protection name is Elizabeth Miller, but my birth name is Kennedy Jane. Yes, I'll hold.'

Beth sits down and turns away from Jonah to face the wall. She leans her head back and looks at the ceiling, the phone held close to her ear.

As he watches her, Jonah's thoughts slow down. How can this be happening? They were so happy this afternoon. Beth's not Jonah's first girlfriend, but she's the first girl he's fallen completely head over heels for. No one has ever set his heart racing or occupied his thoughts like Beth does. He'd give anything to wind back a few hours, to relive that moment they had together, that last kiss before all this began.

That kiss. Jonah knows in his heart it was their last true moment. Once she finds out what he did, or what he didn't do, his role in all of this, she won't want to kiss him like that ever again. The knot in Jonah's stomach tightens. He can't bear the thought of losing Beth. She's everything. She brings out his best. When Jonah is with her he likes who he is, which hasn't always been the case.

The first few years of high school were difficult for Jonah. He lacked confidence and never stood up for himself, making him an easy target. One of the older kids, Paul Silk, had it in for him. Paul was almost twice his size and known to pick a fight. Jonah didn't stand a chance, so he spent most of his time avoiding being anywhere Paul might show up. Jonah was especially scared to walk from school to his mum's work. He'd hang back and make sure he was last to leave, but he hated himself for it. He hated himself for being weak.

One day, Jonah waited and waited until he was sure Paul had gone home before heading off across the oval. Jonah heard the library door open behind him and his heart skipped a beat. But, instead of his tormentor, Beth ran out to catch up with him. She'd been kept back for talking too much in class. She chatted to Jonah all the way across the oval. No wonder she was in trouble for talking, she literally didn't stop.

When they reached the other side of the oval Beth stood in front of him and smiled. 'I'm off to karate now. You should come along sometime, you'd be good at it.'

Beth's invitation took Jonah by surprise. He didn't feel very good at anything. Besides, her old man scared him even more than Paul, but he figured other kids went along to karate and survived, so why not? That night he asked his mum if he could try it.

The next week, Jonah found himself following Beth through the park to the gym after school. She was thrilled to see him and stayed close by during his first session. She was comfortable and familiar with the lesson and that gave him confidence too. It was obvious that Beth had grown up with it. Her movements were fluid, controlled and strong. It was like she was dancing. Beth kept encouraging Jonah and he tried hard because any improvement seemed to please her. It didn't take Jonah long to realise he liked pleasing Beth.

After a few weeks, he realised something else too. He went for hours during the day without thinking about Paul Silk. It was like Beth had opened the secret door to Jonah's confidence, his self-esteem. That combined with a growth spurt was finally enough for Jonah to stand up for himself. The next time Paul shoved him hard in the chest and went to throw a punch, Jonah deflected his fist and grabbed him by the front of the shirt. He walked Paul backwards into the school sports shed and told him to leave him alone. And for whatever reason, it worked. Paul never gave him any trouble again. No one else dared to either. Beth is more than just the girl of his dreams. When Jonah is with her, he is a better version of himself.

Movement on the TV screen catches Jonah's attention. It's Beth's driveway. The van is moving.

'No,' Beth says. 'Mum said not to. I can't disclose that until you're here. What time will they —'

Beth senses something and spins around to see what Jonah's looking at.

'One sec. Can you hold? I'll be back.' Beth drops the phone onto the desk and runs past Jonah to the door. 'Keep watching. Tell me which way they go,' she calls over her shoulder.

The van is in no hurry. It pauses at the cattle grid at the end of the drive and turns left.

'Left,' Jonah yells. 'Beth, they've gone left!'

He hears Beth jump out of the other container and climb up the ladder to the trapdoor. Jonah watches until the van is out of sight, then goes after her.

Beth is standing in the empty dam, a drone beside her. It whirs into action and launches straight up as fast as it can go. Jonah follows the altitude reading on Beth's screen until it reaches 120 metres.

'Maximum flight altitude reached,' the robotic voice announces.

Beth uses the controls to find the van. It's getting dark now but the white van should show up on the screen easily enough.

'How far can it go?' Jonah asks.

'Eight kay,' Beth says.

The van comes into view on Caldwell Lane. Beth breathes in through her nose and out slowly through her mouth, like she does just before a fight. The van slows and turns just before the Youngs' driveway. It follows a track along the fence line and then veers right at a channel junction and crosses at a culvert. It meanders though some trees, passes a large shiny roof, possibly a machinery shed, then parks alongside a much smaller building.

'That's Clive and Gwen's old stable. They're away on holiday,' Beth says.

She zooms in to see the van more clearly on the screen. The side door opens. Two men step down and drag out a body. It's Lucy, Jonah's sure of it. She's dressed in brown camo gear and a black hood covers her head. It's probably the same hood that was on his head. Jonah swallows. He can't watch any longer. Lucy is dead and it's all his fault. He glances at Beth and his heart squeezes in his chest. Because of him, Beth has no mum. How is he going to live with that?

'See that?' Beth says. 'There!'

Jonah doesn't want to see it. He can't live with it. Not now, not ever.

'See that?' Beth is excited.

Jonah brings his eyes down to look at the screen, but he's too late. Lucy is gone.

'Did you see that, Jonah?' Beth says. 'She moved! She moved, Jonah.' Beth grabs his face and kisses him. 'She's alive.'

Jonah doesn't know what to say. He saw how lifeless Lucy's body was with his own eyes. Beth is only seeing what she wants to see. Lucy got shot three times at close range. There's no way she could survive that, surely. Jonah studies Beth's face. He wants to hold her, to tell her what he's done, but he can't. Now's not the right time. He has to hold it together, for her.

THIRTEEN
BETH

As soon as the drone touches the ground I grab it and go.

'C'mon,' I say to Jonah. 'Close the hatch after you.'

'Beth, I'm not sure what you think you saw . . .'

'I'll show you. Quick!'

Jonah comes in as I'm downloading the footage onto the computer.

We watch in double time until the van reaches the stable, then I flick it into slow-motion. I zoom right in and reduce the speed even more. Mum is pulled out of the van by two of the men. She's a dead weight and you can see that they're straining to lift her. Her legs drag behind her until they hit the ground, then her left leg bends and plants firmly on the soil.

'There!' I say. 'She does it again. Keep watching.'

The same foot lifts off the ground, bends at the knee and plants firmly down again.

Jonah sits up and leans forward, concentrating.

'Did you see it?' I say.

'Yes. I saw it.' His hands come up to his face and he looks like he's about to cry. 'I saw it.' He repeats. 'She's alive. Thank God, she's alive.' He pauses and looks at me. 'So what do we do now?'

FOURTEEN
JONAH

Beth picks up the phone. They'd both forgotten they left the police on the line. When Beth holds it to her ear she makes a face.

'They must have hung up. I've changed my mind about calling the local guys,' she says. 'We can't wait for the police from Sydney. They're seven hours away. Mum needs an ambulance now.'

Jonah breathes a sigh of relief. He's glad Beth's finally seeing sense.

Beth taps the receiver button. Once, twice, then hits it repeatedly in frustration.

'The phone's dead.' Her voice falls flat. She replaces the handset and sits down, resting her elbows on the table and probing her forehead with her fingers. 'They must have cut the line. Jesus. What does this mean for us?'

Fear creeps into Jonah's heart as he realises they're alone. No one is coming. No one knows where they are. Lucy and Bear would know what to do, but because of him they're not here. He wants to keep Beth calm, but no words of comfort come. Hopelessness hangs thick in the room.

Jonah feels sick. He sits down. He can't begin to fathom what Beth has been through today, but his ordeal wasn't a walk in the park either. Those men beat him, tied him up and covered his face. After they found his phone it didn't take them long to realise that he wasn't just Bear's student, but Bear's daughter's boyfriend. They kicked and taunted him about what they were going to do to him, what they'd do to Beth and her parents. They weren't going to let him go. He was going to be bait, collateral damage. He owes Beth and Lucy everything for saving him. He has to help them, but what can he do? There has to be something.

Jonah is fit and fast. He could run for help. The van isn't at the house anymore, so he could get Warra's bike and make it back to Trent's place.

Beth looks at Jonah, her jaw clenched with determination.

'We're going to have to do it ourselves. Mum's hurt. We need to get her out now.'

Jonah wants to say something brave, but he can't. Rescuing Lucy would be near impossible.

She's guarded by violent men with guns. Going in there would be suicide. Even if they managed to get Lucy out, then what?

Beth goes to the coffee table, sits opposite Jonah and smooths out a map of the property. Jonah splays his hands on the table to hold it down as Beth lays another clear map of the channels over the top.

'We're here,' Beth says, tapping their position to show Jonah exactly where the bunker is. 'Mum's here.' She taps the table just off the map to roughly indicate the location of the Youngs' old stable. 'If I use the channels as cover they won't see me approaching. This one almost takes me right there.'

Beth leans across the table to squeeze Jonah's hand. The knot in Jonah's stomach tightens. He has to stop all physical contact with Beth until he tells her the truth. It's the only decent thing to do. He moves his hand away, trying to make it look unintentional, but he sees the hurt in her eyes. Beth sits back slowly, drawing away from him.

'Shouldn't we try to make it to a neighbour's place and call the police?' Jonah says quickly.

'The Youngs aren't home. Anyone else is too far. We don't have enough time.'

'I could ride to Trent's place.'

'I don't know. I mean, what if something happened to them too? I think we have to go and rescue her ourselves.'

'Your mum just got shot trying to rescue me, Beth. What if you get hurt too? How am I going to live with that?'

'Jonah, don't –'

Jonah can't take it anymore. He raises his hand to stop Beth midsentence.

'Beth, listen to me, please, this whole thing is my fault. They found you because of me. That photo I posted with your dad, it . . . it was reposted by the International Fight Organisation. They saw it. That's how they knew where to find you. They traced Bear from the photo. When they figured out who I was they thanked me. They told me I led them straight to him, to you.'

Beth stares at Jonah, motionless.

'I told you to take that photo down.'

'I know.' Jonah looks away.

'Fucking hell, Jonah! You knew the rules! Why didn't you take it down?'

'I couldn't see why it was such a big deal.'

'Well, it is, Jonah. And you *lied* to me. You and everyone else. Now look what you've done.'

'How was I to know about all –' Jonah waves his hands around '– THIS? I mean, who hides out for seventeen years? What the fuck did your parents do to these people?' As soon as the words pass through his lips he wishes he could swallow them back up. But that's the thing with words. Once they're said, they are out there forever, fouling the air like a flooded septic tank.

Beth stands up. 'We were in witness protection, Jonah, and I don't know. All THIS is new to me too.' Her eyes well up and she blinks back tears.

'Beth.' Jonah wants to apologise.

'Fuck you, Jonah. Fuck you.'

'I didn't mean . . .'

But she's gone.

Jonah hears her banging around in the other container – cupboard doors opening and closing, zips zipping, clips clipping. She reappears in the doorway wearing black jeans, a black jacket, black boots, a rifle with a scope slung across her chest, ammo belts, explosives, a thigh holster holding a Smith and Wesson .38 revolver and an army camo helmet with night vision. Jonah stares at her, open mouthed.

'I'm going,' she says.

Jonah finds his voice. 'Jesus Christ, Beth. Going out there is suicide and you know it. We should call the police.'

'They've cut the phone lines, Jonah. We don't have time to figure it out.'

'I'll run to a neighbour's place. I'll get my bike from the house and ride to Trent's.'

'Look, you do whatever you want,' Beth says. 'You're good at that.'

Her words sting, but Jonah follows her to the trapdoor. 'You can't just walk around like that. It's illegal to carry all those weapons.'

'You think I care what's legal or not right now?' Beth turns on him. 'You think I care what the police or courts will do *if* I survive this? Those guys have taken everything from me. Everything I have, everything I've ever known, everything I care about. So you do you, Jonah. Call the police, get them out here, do whatever it is you think is the most big-fucking-hero thing to do. But I'm going to get my parents back. I'm going to get my life back.'

And with that, she's gone.

FIFTEEN
BETH

I make my way out of the bunker and into the channel system. I know I don't have much time. Their plan may be to kill me in front of Dad, but what about Mum? What's their plan for her? Will they kill her in front of him too? They may have already done it. It could already be too late.

My pack contains our last two drones and some small explosives. I realise now that the explosives must be left over from when Dad helped people build cyclone and fire bunkers. They could come in handy if I need to create a distraction like Mum did with the tree. Then I realise I haven't actually got a plan. Jonah was right about calling the police. But adding together the time it will take him to make it to a phone and the time it takes police to drive out here, they're over an hour away.

Mum said I've been trained for this day. I can shoot, fight, drive cars and motorbikes, I can fly drones. Heck, I can even use gelignite without blowing myself up. But what about the other things you can't train for? Things like finding a parent dead, seeing a parent die, or looking death in the face yourself. What about taking another human's life? I don't know if I can do any of those things. Could I live with them?

My hands are already clammy. Darkness has set in, but the full moon gives enough light for me to see. I feel for my night vision goggles and pull them down over my eyes. I turn them on to check they are working and the world is suddenly green. I can see well enough without them for now, so I flick them off and shunt them back up to sit on the top of my helmet. As I run, my whole body thrums with nerves. I don't worry about the noise I'm making as my boots splash through the mud. I know where those men are. They are too far away to hear me, and for killers who are supposed to be pros they're pretty slapdash. Something Jonah said plays on my mind. Killing me in front of Dad is personal. Maybe they're not professional hit men after all. Maybe these guys are from Chicago. Professional assassins would have already killed us and been long gone by now. Carlos must be here too. A chill passes over me. I try to ignore it and keep running.

I get into a good rhythm, legs working hard. The first thing that comes into view is the roof of the stable they took Mum into. I duck down below the bank of the channel and twist out of my backpack. The smallest drone is on top. The bottom of the channel is full of water so I have to place it on the bank for take-off. It whirs into action and I send it straight up until I can't see or hear it, muting the robotic voice before it tells me that it has reached its maximum height. As soon as it reaches altitude I thrust it forward towards the old stable.

There's just enough light for me to see the roof of the stable and the white van come into view on my screen. The van is moving slowly towards Clive's machinery shed until it disappears underneath the roof space. They must be hiding it in there. The dark figure of a man walks back to the stables and goes inside. I leave the drone in the sky and watch for a few more seconds. There's no movement so I bring the drone back towards me and lower it down. When it lands all I can think about is what they might be doing to Mum inside that building.

I start running.

SIXTEEN
JONAH

Jonah doesn't know what to do. He's crushed. He knew about Bear's strict social media rules, he just didn't understand the reasons behind them. The adoration on Bear's face in that picture was even better than winning the medal and he wanted everyone in the town to see it. Jonah was over the moon when it got reposted by the International Fight Organisation and he deliberately didn't tell Beth. But that's where those men saw it. They taunted Jonah as they bound his hands and feet, congratulating him for making their job so easy. And now they have Lucy.

Jonah watches Beth's head bobbing along the cross channel towards Caldwell Lane. He wants to call out to her but he doesn't dare. He wants to scream. Why did he say that about her parents?

Why did he post that photo? Jonah tries to think clearly. There must be another way to contact the police. There's no infrastructure out here for communication devices, but a sat phone would work. Surely Lucy and Bear would have one in the bunker. Jonah searches both containers but doesn't find anything. By the time Jonah arms himself and climbs back out of the bunker to follow Beth it's too late. She's long gone.

Jonah stands in the dry dam and looks up at the large round moon. There's no way he can ever make up for this monumental mistake, but he has to do something. Should he go after Beth in case she needs help? Or should he see if he can reach the house to get Warra's bike and ride for help? Would any of those men still be there?

Jonah kicks the weeds by the trapdoor in frustration. Letting Beth run off alone has put him in a terrible position. If he goes after her and is caught again, he is certain those guys will kill him. They could all be captured and then they'd have no hope of surviving. The most sensible thing to do would be to get Warra's bike and ride to Trent's. Even if it's an hour before the police arrive.

But Beth could be captured and killed by then, and Lucy was shot risking her life to save him. If nothing slowed her down, Beth would have arrived at the old stable by now — they may already have her. There's no way he can run in the opposite direction, no matter how he tries to justify it. He has to go after Beth. He has to try to help her save Lucy.

Jonah closes the trapdoor and crawls out through the pipe into the channel. He leaves the stop beside the pipe and runs.

SEVENTEEN
BETH

I crouch behind the machinery shed and pause for a few seconds before sneaking in. Two feral cats dart away to hide among the old header and trucks as I enter. I take a moment to gather my thoughts. First, I need to find out if Mum is still alive and if Dad is here too.

I sneak back out of the machinery shed the same way I entered. There's a clearing between here and the stable. If anyone walks out while I'm approaching I'll be seen.

The voices of two men drift across from the stable, getting louder. I notice they have American accents. I run back into the shed, where it's darker with plenty of places to hide. I duck under the old header, crouching behind the wheels so I can't be seen. Fear explodes inside me and I have to concentrate on my breathing to keep it quiet. The men come into view. One of them has a bandage on his hand. It's soaked with blood.

'Are you sure?' the other man asks him.

'Of course. What is this? You suddenly don't trust me?'

'We just don't want to be taking our time if the cops are on the way.'

'There are no phones working within a fifty-mile radius of this joint. I took the old pick-up truck and cut the line while you three were at the house. They can't pick up service on a cell way out here. We have plenty of time to find the girl.'

A loud bang comes from behind me. It must be one of the feral cats. I slowly bring my hand to my gun and rest my thumb above the holster clip. My heart pounds hard, but I manage to keep my breathing steady.

The men stop walking and draw their guns and flashlights. I have nowhere to go. Black boots appear beside me. They creep forward. I try to get further behind the tyres, but every time I move I make a scuffing noise on the concrete floor. The men stop. I freeze. But I'm not in a good position. If they crouch down, they'll see me.

A cat darts towards the men. It runs past them and out the front of the shed. The men laugh, one of them making a screeching noise to imitate the startled animal. They chide each other as one gets into the van. He reverses out. The guy with the bandage on his hand grabs something out of the back then walks over to the old stable and goes inside. A different man comes out, jumps into the passenger seat and finally the van moves off down the driveway. This is better for me. If I've counted right, with two men gone, there are only two left inside the stable for me to deal with.

A spectacular orange moon sits above the horizon and brings me hope. I pull down my night vision goggles and turn them on. The world turns green.

Staying behind the tree line, I circle the stable, going the long way round. I want to scout out the situation from all angles before I decide what I'm going to do. I make it the whole way around and see nothing. No sign of the men and no sign of Mum or Dad. Clive's old digger, the one that Gwen calls the 'big yellow shovel', is parked at the back of the building. I decide to try and make it to that machine. It will get me closer and give me good cover from sight and gunfire.

I creep, I stalk, I run. I edge nearer. *Patience is everything. Make sure it's safe, and never advance in haste.* Dad's words come back to me from when we played combat games with paintball guns out in the bush. Whenever I'd get sick of waiting, sick of going slow, I'd get shot. I soon learned patience. Only this isn't paintball and my heart knows the difference. It's galloping in my chest. I have to psych myself into sprinting the last little distance. I breathe deeply.

In through my nose, count to ten, then out through my mouth. I roll my shoulders to loosen them up and shake out the nervous tension in my legs. All the things I do before a big fight. Mum said I'm ready for this. I'm ready.

With that final thought I take off; springy quiet toes, gentle landings, no thudding of boots. I move swiftly and silently until I'm pressed against the big yellow shovel. I stand still, catching my breath, calming myself down.

A voice inside the stable reaches me. It's loud and full of anger.

'Where is she?'

Silence.

'Even if you don't talk, my men will find her eventually. No one is coming to save you. You will watch her die. Then you will know what it feels like to see the life drain from your own flesh and blood, unable to help them, unable to save them. She will die like a frightened animal and you will see every second of it. You will suffer like I suffered when you killed my son.'

'No!' It's Mum. She screams the word with rage. Her voice is pained but she's still alive.

I need to know how many men are in there with her and whether they have guns. I move closer to the tin wall of the stable and find small nail holes to peek through. My view is restricted, but through my night vision I can see Mum in a chair, slumped forward. Her hands are tied behind her back. Beside her I can see part of Dad's arm, it's unmistakable. My heart leaps with hope. They're both there.

It looks like Dad's hands are pulled behind him and tied too. The man with a bandaged hand walks into view holding a revolver. He has shockingly white hair and is wearing black cargo pants and a black shirt with the sleeves rolled up. He extends his arm, his gun only an inch away from Mum's head, pointed directly at her face.

I pull away. I can't watch.

'Where is she?' He keeps asking the same question over and over. I can hear Mum whimpering, like he might be hurting her. I have to move fast. I scuttle up to the driver's seat of the old digger and pray that it has a battery in it. The key's in the ignition. The engine turns over, then stops. I try again. This time it winds down like the battery is going flat.

Oh no. I pull the choke.

I try the key again, then I aim my rifle at a part of the stable wall I know isn't near where my parents are and I fire. I fire again. Then I reload and fire a third time so they won't come charging around the back while I get the machine moving. The engine roars to life and shunts forward when I put it into gear. I rev it hard. The louder it is the bigger it feels. I load my rifle again and fire. I need them to be taking cover, not returning fire. I drive straight through the back wall of the stable. The posts crack and tin rips apart. I put my foot down and charge forward, taking part of the wall with me. I fire my gun again as I pull up near Dad. None of the men are in sight. I spring down, knife in hand, and land right beside him. I slice through Dad's hand tie and pass him the knife. He moves fast. He unties Mum, picks her up and throws her over his shoulder. I fire another shot as he makes his way out the back of the building. There's yelling, return fire and pockmarks spatter the tin wall beside me. I can't see where they're hiding but I shoot a few more rounds around the shed and back out after Dad. He's making his way towards the machinery shed. I catch up as fast as I can and pass him my handgun.

'Is the bunker secure?' he asks.

'Yes.'

'Run ahead, Beth.'

Gunfire sounds behind us. I peel off to the side and roll onto the ground, flat on my stomach. I use my elbow to stabilise my gun and fire. Dad keeps moving. I cover him while he runs towards the shed, then he covers me while I run to join him.

I twist my pack around to my front, reach inside and pull out another set of night vision goggles for Dad. He places them around his head and adjusts the straps. He picks up Mum again and places her across his shoulders. Then, with gunfire and the roar of the old digger's engine behind us, we head for the channel.

EIGHTEEN
JONAH

Rapid gunfire sounds over the roar of a large machine. Jonah stops to listen, refusing to think what those shots might mean. Then he hears something else, a smaller engine approaching from the road. Jonah reckons he's got about thirty seconds before the vehicle comes into view and the driver can see him. Out here, the landscape is so flat and barren that any movement could catch their eye. The moonlight is bright and he's still in his karate uniform – but maybe he has a chance? He lies flat against the bank of the channel and doesn't move a muscle. The white van slows as it crosses the culvert, the tail-lights glowing red. Jonah holds his position, his heart hammering. He doesn't want to get caught again. He can't. He wishes he could run as fast as he could away from all this and not turn back, but he won't. He can't abandon Beth. The van moves on. They didn't see him. Jonah exhales slowly then presses forward, keeping low. He's making good time. One more bend and he'll be running parallel with Caldwell Lane. The slush makes the run hard, but he's been through worse on Bear's survival camps. He doesn't care about the mud or leeches.

Jonah can't imagine anyone taking Bear hostage. He's a huge man, strong and fit with muscles on muscles. But his mind is even tougher than his body. Pure grit. He never gives up. Those men must have caught him completely unaware, or maybe they drugged him with something.

Beth said he was some kind of agent in America. It all makes sense now. All of his rules, all of the classes he runs. All the things Carly thought were weird crazy-man stuff. Turns out there was a reason for them after all. Survival. He was equipping Beth to survive no matter what her future held. Jonah can't imagine having to leave his home, never to see or hear from anyone in his life again. Not to be Jonah Keath anymore. How would he feel about that? How does Beth feel now?

Jonah kicks himself. He should have told Beth he loves her no matter what her name is. No matter what her parents did. No matter what happens.

He should have told her.

Jonah rounds the bend and feels some of the tension in his chest release. He feels a little safer, for now anyway, running in the channel parallel with the main road. At least he can't be seen. Picking up speed, Jonah prays that those shots had nothing to do with Beth and that he arrives before she tries anything. He needs to let her know he's here, that he didn't leave her, that he's come to help even though they'll probably all be killed. He pushes away awful thoughts of her being captured. Those men talked about Beth in front of him . . . If they catch her they will kill her. What if he's already too late?

Suddenly, Jonah hears movement in the darkness ahead. He freezes. Jesus. Fuck. What if it's the guys from the van? Maybe they did see him after all. He runs straight up and over the bank, hoping they haven't spotted him yet. He rolls until he finds a ditch, allows himself to fall into it and doesn't move. The footsteps get louder, closer. There are no voices, just the sound of their feet. It's hard to tell how many people there are, but there's definitely more than one. Could it be Beth and Lucy? Has Beth already rescued her? He's not game enough to check. He stays down, flat against the ground. The people in the channel run by and move further away. It could have been the Millers . . . but Jonah has no way of knowing for sure. When he thinks it's safe to get up, he scrambles back into the channel and keeps running towards the old stable.

When Jonah arrives there's chaos. One of the stable walls is smashed in and damaged. Men are yelling over the sound of an engine roaring. It appears Beth has completed her rescue, a brazen one at that. Jonah laughs to himself. Go Beth.

'They're in the channels,' one man screams.

'Flush them out!' another answers.

It must have been Beth and Lucy that passed him earlier. Maybe Bear too. Jonah could cry with relief. They would have made it back to the bunker by now, and no one would think to look for them at the bottom of a dry dam. At least they'll be safe while he runs for help.

Jonah slinks back down into the channel. He knows it's no longer safe to use them as cover, but the open paddocks aren't any safer. He starts to move quickly back the way he came to put some distance between himself and the men at the stable. As soon as he can he'll get out and find another way get to Trent's place to call for help.

NINETEEN
BETH

The three of us reach the pipe that runs into the dry dam but this time we don't use it. With Dad holding Mum it's too narrow. I throw my bag up onto the bank and then help Dad carry Mum into the basin and manoeuvre her through the trapdoor.

Dad carries Mum down the ladder and places her gently on the ground. I follow, securing the trapdoor behind me. Dad runs into the storage container and comes back with a camp bed and roll-out mattress. He sets it up just outside the doorway of the operational container and comes back for Mum. He carries her to the stretcher and lays her down. He fetches her water and pain relief tablets. She takes them and settles down on the stretcher. Dad cuts off her ballistic vest and pulls it out from under her. The bruising is already dark purple over one side of her chest and down her ribs. The journey from the stable on Dad's shoulders would have been agonising.

'Grab an icepack from the fridge,' Dad says as he tries to make her comfortable. 'I'm so sorry I had to carry you like that,' he says to Mum.

'You did good,' Mum whispers. 'Thank you.' Her fingers wrap around his and tears come to her eyes.

I move as fast as I can. It looks so painful. Mum winces with every movement, every breath.

'Do you think your ribs are broken?' I say, wrapping the cold pack in a tea towel and pressing it against Mum's side.

'Yeah, I'd say so,' she replies. Her words come out breathy, as though asserting any greater effort to speak would finish her off. 'I'm better now that I'm back here.' Tears streak down her face.

My tears start and I can't stop them. Mum's and Dad's faces are bruised and swollen from being bashed. They have blood all over them. Even though I am a trained fighter, I can't imagine hitting someone with such brutality. Suddenly, I realise Jonah's gone. He must have tried to make it to Trent's.

'Easy now,' Dad says.

'You've got to go,' Mum whispers. 'Take Beth and get out of here.'

Dad shakes his head. 'We're not leaving you here.'

'No way,' I say. 'We stick together. We're safe down here.'

'They want Beth,' Mum says to Dad. 'Get her out.'

Dad glances at me.

'I already know,' I say. 'Jonah told me. It's not fair. I had nothing to do with what happened in Chicago.'

Mum looks at me. 'It's his ultimate revenge. Carlos is a sick man,' she murmurs.

'I need to know what happened back then, so I understand what's going on now. You have to tell me.'

Mum and Dad look at each other.

'What did you do?' I persist. They're silent for a minute. I wait. I need to know.

Mum tries to sit up, wincing in pain. Dad places his hands on her shoulders and gently guides her back down onto the stretcher.

'I'll handle it,' he says.

Mum nods. Tears slide down her cheeks and land on the pillow.

'Tell her everything, Bear. Everything. She has a right to know,' she says.

Dad nods. He waves me inside the first container. 'Take a seat, Beth.'

We sit down on the old red leather couch.

'Before you were born, your mum and I worked together in America . . .'

I nod for him to continue. Dad doesn't know what Mum's already told me, and I don't tell him. I need to hear everything again.

'We worked for the government in intelligence and surveillance,' he continues. 'Some of it was dangerous work. There was a drug ring that we'd been watching for a long time. We had reason to believe that Carlos and his family were big players. We'd had an undercover operative in among them for eighteen months and it was finally time to do our raid and make the arrests. I was in charge, the one calling the shots. Your mother and . . . er –' he coughs '– others were involved too.'

I frown. 'Others?'

Dad ignores my question and keeps going. 'Our undercover operative had a wire and went to Carlos's house to buy the gear. Our plan was to bust in, seize the drugs and arrest the key players. Only things didn't go to plan. Then everything happened so fast. There was no time to think . . .'

Dad pauses before continuing. 'Carlos worked with two of his sons but the third, the youngest, wasn't involved. He was entirely innocent, didn't know anything about his family's drug business yet. He was about your age now and no one expected him to be there. He was supposed to be at a mate's house but, kids being kids, he'd snuck back home to raid the grog stash and walked in on the deal. There was confusion and yelling . . . My focus was on getting our guy out. He called for us to hold off, but blew his cover in the process. I couldn't leave him in there after that. We had already arrested and charged others in their circle. They would have killed him without hesitation. So I made the decision to go in. I gave the order. Our operative was shot and killed in the crossfire and so was the kid. It was the wrong call and something I've had to live with ever since. Their blood is on my hands and I can never wash it away.'

Dad holds his head between his hands and massages his temples. He sighs. 'The others were charged and put away, but even with Carlos behind bars we received threats. We had no choice but to go into witness protection. He's a powerful man and has connections. When his sons got out of jail they wanted nothing more to do with him. His wife left him too. He lost his business, his family, and he blames me for all of it. There are three hit men here with him that he's been working with in Chicago for a long time. He wants to kill you because he wants me to suffer the same fate as he did. He's driven and ruthless and clearly put a lot of time and energy into finding us and plotting this sick revenge. My guess is that it's what's kept him going. He's very danger- ous, Beth.'

'He really wants to make you watch me die?'

'Yes,' Dad says, 'I don't doubt that.'

'And what about the family of the undercover guy?'

Dad's gaze drops to the floor. I can tell this still pains him. 'They were devastated.' He closes his eyes at the memory. 'I'm not sure they know the full truth about what happened that day.'

It all weighs heavily on my chest. The burden of this awful mistake on Dad, how it changed his life, cut him off from friends and family, his work. I get who Dad is now. I finally *get* him. The survival courses, the firearms training, the self-defence classes . . . His intense drive and focus. He wasn't being over-protective of me at all. He knew the threat was out there. People at school and in town often judged him for being too strict with me, behind his back, of course, because no one would ever be game to say something to his face. If only they'd known who he really was and what he'd been through. They wouldn't have thought he was a gung-ho maniac at all. He's just a normal dad protecting his family the best way he knows how.

'They caught me off-guard in town,' says Dad, 'but you should've seen the look on their faces when you crashed through the wall in the digger, all kitted up. They weren't expecting that.'

It breaks the mood and we both laugh.

'You did good, kiddo. I'm proud of you.'

'I was so scared,' I say. My voice cracks. 'I didn't know you were there, but I knew they had Mum. I was scared I'd be too late.'

Dad reaches over to hug me and we're quiet for a moment.

'Mum told me my real name,' I say. 'But I don't know yours.'

Dad smiles and his shoulders drop, like some long-held pressure is released from him.

'Leo Jane.' It rolls off his tongue like he's said it a million times before, yet I've never heard those two names said together. 'Your mum is Brendena Patrick.'

The names sound so foreign that they don't sink in at first. Leo and Brendena. Brendena Patrick. I say their names in my head. Then I add mine. Leo, Brendena and Kennedy. The Jane-Patrick family. Or would it be Patrick-Jane?

'Are you married?'

'No. We never got married and once we left it was too late, even if we wanted to.'

I don't know how to feel about this. I know it makes no difference. People don't need to make vows or have a piece of paper to legitimise a relationship, but it's weird to think of my parents in a different light to how I've always thought of them.

Mum groans. Dad is up on his feet and out to her in a flash.

He comes back to grab another glass of water then holds it to her lips. She sips at it and settles back down, favouring one side. I'm standing at the doorway watching him. His love and devotion to her is as clear as day and I realise how lucky I am to have grown up with that in my life. That is real.

I sit back down on the couch and leave my parents to themselves for a while. We should probably be working out our next plan of attack. Mum needs a doctor.

Dad appears in the doorway.

'Mum just asked where Jonah is.'

He says it like it's a statement but I know it's really a question. I sit up and look Dad square in the face.

'He said he was going to try to get help. He would have gone to the Grangers. I really hope he's okay.' I pause. 'He's my boyfriend.' My lips curl up as I say it and I feel myself blushing. 'It's been six weeks. I was going to tell you today after school but you disappeared.'

'So it's serious, huh?'

'Well, we've always been good friends, and I . . .' I feel awkward talking to Dad about this. 'It's not just a passing crush if that's what you want to know. It's much more than that. We want to be together.'

Dad sits down.

'Mum said he was here? Does she mean here in the bunker?'

'Yes. When we didn't turn up at training he got worried. He came out to make sure I was okay. Those men got him and . . .' I swallow. 'Mum and I went to rescue him and that's when they shot her. Then they must have cut the phone lines because we lost connection. We kind of freaked out a bit and got into a fight.' A fat tear moves down my cheek and I push it away. 'I stormed off to rescue Mum and left him here. He must have gone to get help. I just hope he's safe.'

'He came here to the bunker?'

'Yes.'

Dad sighs.

'What?'

'He's a liability. If he gets caught again he'll tell them where we are.'

'No, he'd never do that.'

Dad goes to say something and stops. But he doesn't have to say it. It slowly dawns on me – they'd torture it out of him. I feel sick at the thought.

TWENTY
JONAH

Jonah lies flat in the paddock near Beth's house as the headlights of the van sweep over him again. The moon is full and the night is light, so he doesn't dare move in case he catches their eye. The white van drives towards the house, crosses the cattle pit and meanders towards the Millers' machinery shed, making sure to shine the headlights into it. Carlos's men are searching for them. They must know they're still on the property. Jonah stays put, deciding what to do. He's heading for the house because Warra's bike is there, but Carlos's men must suspect the Millers will come back for something too. Maybe they think they're hiding close by.

The van stops. A man gets out and walks into the shed to look at something. Just as Jonah decides to get up and make a run for it, the man gets back into the van and it moves off again. The van drives towards the house, sweeps its high beams across the windows and then slowly turns around and rolls back down the driveway. Jonah lies still, doesn't even breathe. His heart thuds so hard he can feel it in his stomach where he presses into the ground. Again, the van swings towards the paddock so the lights shine across it. Did they see him? He turns his face into the dirt, away from the van, so the light doesn't catch the gleam of his eyes.

The van stops moving for what feels like forever. Can they see something? Maybe they're not sure what it is, or maybe they're waiting to see if it moves. Do they have him in their sights? Jonah can't hold his breath any longer. He slowly draws in air and waits, not knowing if a gunshot will be the last thing he hears. Finally the light slides away from him and the van drives on.

Jonah decides going to the house for the bike is too risky. They might notice it's gone and start dropping into the neighbouring properties to look for him. Beth said they'd kill anyone who gets in their way. Jonah doesn't want anything to happen to the Grangers.

Jonah is going to have to get to Trent's place through the paddocks. If these guys are patrolling the roads, they might be looking for footprints. It will be slower and harder work, but it's better than being caught again. He's familiar with the country out here and Bear has given him enough survival and combat training for him to know not to lose his head and do things in haste.

When the van is far enough away, Jonah gets up off the ground and makes a dash for the trees that run along Caldwell Lane. He goes over the fence into the Frankels' rice stubble. Then, with the full moon shining brightly above him, he starts running.

The night air is cold on Jonah's face as he strides out. It's difficult terrain underfoot. The ground is hard and uneven. He stumbles a couple of times but recovers. After what must be a few kilometres of jogging through paddocks and up and down banks, Jonah's legs start to burn. He pushes through it and tries to run faster. He keeps his eyes on the ground so he doesn't miss a pot hole or a hard clod that could send him sailing. Then he hears a shot. He whips his head up and looks in the direction it came from. The ground disappears beneath him, his foot goes into a hole but his momentum keeps the rest of his body moving forward. The earth grabs his foot and he goes down hard. As he falls his foot rolls and he feels something inside his ankle give. White-hot pain shoots out from where his ankle gave way as he slams onto the ground. He knows it's bad. Another shot sounds. Pain fills his lower leg, but he doesn't dare cry out. He lies still, gasping for air, scanning his surrounds for the van, for men with guns. They could be anywhere. He waits but hears nothing.

He drags his injured foot closer. The pain moving it is excruciating.

Fuck, fuck, FUCK! He punches the ground. This could be the thing that gets him killed.

He reins in his fear, his fury, his frustration. He has to keep a clear head. Bear taught him that. When things go wrong people die because they panic. They die because they lose their cool. He is not those people. He can do this. He can still make it to the Grangers' place.

Jonah grits his teeth and stands with his weight on his good foot. The injured one feels okay. He doesn't think it's broken, but as soon as he places it on the ground he's in a world of pain. It's unable to bear weight. He hops forward, then gently places his foot down. He shuffles his good foot forward then does it again, refusing to think about how long it might take him to reach the Grangers' farm, refusing to think about how he will not be able to run away if the men with guns find him.

Every step is progress.

TWENTY-ONE
BETH

'They won't catch him,' I say. 'If he left when I did he would have been at the Granger's place before we even got back here.' But then I think of the two men who left before I rescued Mum and Dad. What if they found him? He could be in trouble again.

Dad massages his temples and lets out a long breath. 'In any case, we can't move Mum right now and I'm not leaving her here alone. She needs an ambulance.'

'I could go.'

'No, Beth. Absolutely not. I'm in two minds. I want to stay and monitor your mum's condition for a couple of hours, but at the same time I don't want to wait in case she deteriorates. Mum made me promise I wouldn't leave without you, but I'm not leaving her here on her own either.'

'Jonah will come through for us,' I say. 'He'll get the police and ambulance out here.' But I'm not convinced, just like Dad isn't.

'For now, try to get some rest,' he says. 'Restore some energy. We don't know what's ahead.'

Now that I'm safe and warm the exhaustion is hitting me. Everything happened so fast, but now the adrenaline has worn off. I lie down on the sofa, but every time I close my eyes I see myself on the digger, busting through the wall of the stable to find Mum and Dad tied to their chairs, beaten and bloodied. I hear our feet sloshing beneath us as we run, I feel the breathlessness, then I taste the fear all over again. I'm glad I'm in a bunker – underground with no windows, only one door – where no one can find us. I wouldn't feel safe anywhere else, knowing those men are still out there.

My thoughts drift to Jonah. A few hours ago our only concern was us. Getting together, staying together, telling Dad so we could achieve those things. I see myself in the park with him, giggling and flushed, nervous and excited, and it makes me sad. We seemed younger then.

I realise Jonah's life changed today too. He was captured, bound, beaten and discovered his girl-friend isn't who he thought she was. I wonder if he's okay. What is he feeling now? My heart aches when I think of him. He came out to see if I was all right. It was sweet and brave. But that was earlier, when bravery meant facing my dad. Now that we are facing four brutal murderers, bravery means something completely different. And to make it worse, Jonah feels responsible for all of this – us being found, Mum getting shot – he's hurting too. Although I'm still angry with him, I wish I could tell him that it's okay, that the rescue was a success and now we are all together and safe in the bunker. I keep telling myself that he made it to Trent's, but my stomach churns not knowing.

I think about Trent and how his violent episode at the hospital changed everything for his family. It didn't just mess up Trent, it destroyed his parents too. People started treating them differently. It makes me wonder, even if we do survive this and the threat of Carlos goes away, could we stay here? For us, being found is also being exposed. When everyone finds out that our whole life in Deni has been a lie, could they ever trust us again? Will they still like and accept us? I wonder how all of my friends will feel about me in the morning, when they find out I'm not Beth Miller anymore. Will they still be friends with me? Will they like Kennedy Jane?

Sleep won't come, so I sit up and look around me. This bunker. Its solid walls and floor. Concrete, literally. It's amazing. It's proof that Mum and Dad knew their past would eventually catch up with them.

That this man, hell-bent on revenge, would never stop looking for them. The lengths taken by my parents to hide us blows my mind. They chose an isolated location on the other side of the world, then did everything they could to blend into a new community and raise me with the necessary skills to survive. And they did all this while maintaining the illusion of a safe, free and happy childhood. The happy was real too. Carlos and those men can't take that away from me.

This last thought makes me stop thinking about what's changed and focus on what has stayed the same instead. What did I have yesterday that I still have today?

Love. The love between me and my parents is pure and unconditional. Even if they kill us, they cannot change or obliterate that.

What else? My genes. I am who I am, even if I was to be disfigured. I have dark eyes like Dad. My hair is golden. I'm tall, almost six foot, and athletic, strong and fit. It's possible for them to change how I look, but they cannot erase my inherited genetics, who I am.

I also have my childhood. Everything that has happened up until this day has not and cannot be taken away from me. No one can change or delete my memories.

And my parents. Who my mother and my father are cannot be changed.

Taking stock of the unchangeable things I have makes me feel better. It makes me realise that I haven't lost everything. The important things are still the same. The things that make me, me.

My thoughts drift to America. I wonder what my life might have been like had that botched raid never happened. Who would that Kennedy Jane have been? Who are her extended family? Would there have been grandparents, aunts, uncles and cousins? I've always felt such a strong pull towards America. I love watching American movies and TV shows just to see different parts of the country. Maybe this isn't a coincidence. Maybe I remember something from when I was a baby, or maybe my parents unwittingly instilled something in me when I was little and they didn't have to pretend so hard to be Australian.

Everything that has happened over the past twenty-four hours and what it means is far greater than my brain can process. It's too large to view all at once, like the sky or the horizon. When I turn to see something, I lose sight of something else.

Dad interrupts my thoughts as he walks past on his way to the bathroom. He's in there for ages and when he finally emerges the blood on his face is cleaned up and there are black stitches holding the cut on his cheek together. I wince at the thought of him stitching himself up.

'What do we do now?' I ask.

'We wait,' says Dad. 'Our plan all along was to get the three of us here, where we can sit out the threat. Mum's already notified our Australian contact, so someone will be on their way. Jonah's also gone for help, which is too dangerous for my liking, but we can't do anything about that now.' Dad walks past me and comes back a minute later holding bags of packaged food. He goes to the kitchenette, takes out a saucepan and half fills it with water. 'Mum seems to have settled and her colour is looking better. I think we just have to sit tight, hope Jonah made it and wait it out for now.'

'What about Carlos and those men?'

Dad empties two packets of dried pasta and some red powder into the water and stirs. I walk over and lean against the kitchen counter so we can talk more easily.

'My main focus right now is to keep you and Mum safe, and our best option is staying here. We'll only move Mum if she's going to the hospital.'

'I could go for help,' I say. 'I know I've said it before, but I could take a car. I could make it into town, I know it.'

'You don't know who you're dealing with, Beth. These people have no respect for authority and no respect for human life. It's not a risk I'm willing to take.'

I look at the bruising on Dad's face.

'Their ultimate punishment for me was to watch you die, and that's the only reason I'm still alive.

There'll be no second chances if they catch us again. Things haven't gone to plan for us, but they haven't gone to plan for Carlos either. He's desperate. Those men will kill us on sight now, if they get the chance.'

The hairs on the back of my neck rise and the prickly feeling spreads down my arms. To hear Dad talk so pragmatically about those men killing us is sickening.

'So, you and Jonah Keath, huh?' says Dad, changing the subject.

I smile wryly at Dad's teasing, but my heart aches at the mention of Jonah. I push into my eyes with my fingers, wiping tears away.

'That was . . . when I was still Elizabeth Miller. When things were simpler. What will they do to Jonah if they catch him?'

Dad removes the pot from the stove top and hugs me.

'He will have made it to a phone by now.'

I rest my head on Dad's shoulder. 'I hope so.'

'I'm sorry this has happened, Beth. Mum and I didn't know when to tell you, or if we should ever tell you. I'm certainly glad they took this long to find us. You're practically an adult now. Smart, strong, resilient. I know it's all come as a huge shock, but we're going to get through this, and we'll do it together. You can handle anything life throws at you. I know you can.'

I let Dad hold me and draw comfort from his words. Even though I understand why they didn't tell me, it still hurts that they decided not to. There have been so many opportunities; every time I asked why I couldn't put photos of us on social media, the reason why certain sports and classes were non-negotiable . . . But could I have handled finding out I wasn't Elizabeth Miller when I was thirteen? Can I handle it now that I'm seventeen? I don't know. I guess I have no choice but to find a way.

Dad serves us dinner and once I start eating I realise how hungry I am. When we've finished I sit down beside Mum and take her hand.

'Are you okay?' I ask. 'Does it hurt?'

Mum nods. 'I'm okay,' she says, but there's no strength in her voice.

'You sound short of breath.'

'A bit,' Mum murmurs.

Dad takes her other hand. 'You're short of breath?' he asks.

Mum nods.

'You said you notified our contact?'

She nods again.

'We wouldn't be on any database here, so they won't know who we are, but they may have seen where you were calling from and already notified the local police. If they did that someone may already be on their way. We might not have to wait much longer. As soon as they're here we'll get you to a hospital.'

'We never gave them our exact location,' I say. 'How will we know when they arrive?'

'I'll do reconnaissance,' says Dad.

'I'll come with you.'

Mum and Dad look at me. 'No,' they say together.

'Now that you're down here, you stay down here until there's no threat up there,' says Dad.

I sigh. This must be how the Queen feels, or the President of the United States. People with bodyguards risking their lives to keep them safe. But it's not quite the same. Those bodyguards are specially trained and paid to put their lives on the line. Mum and Dad are specially trained too, but they're protecting me out of love. Even if they weren't trained they'd still take a bullet for me. Any parent would. Love is a powerful force. I think of Carlos. In his case, the loss of a loved one is what's driving his hatred, his revenge, but ultimately he is still risking his life and freedom for love. Maybe love is the most powerful force on the planet after all. Or could it be hatred? I remember how I felt driving through the wall of the stable to save Mum. My desperation, my rage. Maybe I'm not so different to Carlos.

I bring out another mattress from the storage container and set it up next to Mum's. Dad does the same on her other side. Sleep doesn't come easily, but eventually I doze off.

TWENTY-TWO
JONAH

When Jonah reaches Trent's driveway he holds the gate for a few seconds, then keeps limping. His injured ankle throbs heavily and his good leg burns with lactic acid and strain. It's still a few kays to go. Jonah pushes away unwanted thoughts about never arriving, about how far it is, and does his best to shut out the pain. Finally Jonah sees the house through the trees, the roof illuminated in the moonlight. He pushes himself to go faster, panic caught tightly in his throat.

Jonah opens the front gate and a kelpie barks and bounds towards him.

'Hey, boy, I'm friendly,' Jonah says. He bends down to scratch the dog's ears and keeps hobbling along. The porch light comes on when he's in range of the sensor.

He stands on the front step of the house and knocks on the door. It's late and the house is quiet. The Grangers are obviously in bed. Jonah knocks again, louder this time. Footsteps sound as someone inside approaches. The door swings back. Carol Granger stands in her dressing gown, securing the belt at her waist.

'Oh . . .' Carol is shocked to see Jonah. She looks him up and down. He's a mess. Carol's eyebrows knit in confusion and she looks past Jonah into the darkness, then back at Jonah. 'Jonah, what are you doing out here at this hour?'

Jonah leans uncomfortably on the doorjamb and can't stop the memory of him and his mum berating this woman in the street from flashing through his mind. What an arrogant shit he was. His cheeks burn.

'I'm really sorry to disturb you, Mrs Granger, but it's an emergency,' Jonah says. 'Could I use your phone, please? The Millers are in trouble and I need to call the police.'

Carol's face softens. 'Our phone isn't working,' she says. 'It went out hours ago. We're not sure why yet. I thought I'd go into town and report it tomorrow.'

Jonah can't believe it. The helplessness of the situation finally crashes down on him and he starts crying.

'What's wrong?' says Carol, alarmed. 'Come in and sit down.'

Jonah goes to move.

'You're hurt,' Carol says. She steps out and ducks under Jonah's arm to help usher him inside as Trent comes down the hallway. He slows when he sees Jonah.

Trent helps his mum lower Jonah onto the sofa.

'What's going on?' Trent asks.

'Jonah's hurt,' Carol says. 'Grab an icepack from the freezer. Bring the first-aid kit too.'

'The Millers need help,' Jonah blurts out. 'Men came with guns.'

'What?' Carol frowns in disbelief.

Trent returns from the kitchen and tends to Jonah's ankle with the icepack. Carol fetches Jonah a glass of water then sits down next to him on the sofa. She makes him tell her the whole story from the beginning. When Jonah's finished, there's a moment's silence before Carol gets to her feet.

'We'll drive into town and get the police imme-diately,' she says.

'I have to go back in case they need help,' Jonah says.

'You will do no such thing,' Carol says. 'You're both coming with me.'

'No, I have to go back. All of this is my fault. I have to make sure they're okay.'

'Jonah, you can hardly walk. You need that ankle strapped. Besides, I will not allow you to go back there by yourself. It's far too dangerous.'

'Then I'll wait here until the police come. I need to be out here so I can show the police where the Millers are hiding. What if they make me stay in town or drive me home? They'll never find the bunker unless I'm here to show them.'

'I could strap his ankle here while we're waiting for you to come back,' says Trent. 'It doesn't look broken but he needs to keep it elevated.'

'Please . . .' Jonah says.

Carol thinks about it. 'Okay. That would probably be helpful, but I want you to promise you'll wait for the police. Trent, you stay with Jonah and don't let him go anywhere until I'm back.'

Trent agrees and Carol leaves to get changed. When she returns she grabs her bag before heading out the door.

It's half an hour in, then half an hour out, plus whatever time it takes to talk to the police and convince them to come. Jonah sits up.

'I'm not sure I can wait,' he says.

'Sounds like you should keep the hell away to me,' says Trent. He gets up and crouches by Jonah to start strapping his ankle.

Jonah scowls, but knows that Trent is right. If he hadn't shown up, Lucy wouldn't have got shot and Beth wouldn't have rushed off on her own. Lucy would have known what to do to keep Beth safe.

But Jonah has to go back. He needs to make up for the trouble he's caused and help in whatever small way he can. If he could just turn up at the right time, he might be able to do something useful.

'They might need help now,' Jonah says.

'No offence, but it doesn't sound like you've been much help so far, mate.'

Jonah glares at Trent.

'It all makes sense now, doesn't it?' Trent says, ignoring Jonah's death stare.

'What?'

'Bear. That man's a fucking giant. Whoever's after them must really mean business.'

Jonah thinks back to when he was being held facedown on the ground, bound with a hood over his head. What the men had been bragging about.

'They were keeping Bear alive so they could see his face when . . .' Jonah struggles to say it. 'When they killed Beth.'

Trent moves his head back in disgust. 'Those sick fucks. That's why you want to go back?'

Jonah nods.

'Well, mate, I'm not stopping you. I know what it's like to live with regret. It grows inside you like a disease, only it doesn't attack your body, it attacks your soul. You can't run away from it. I'd never wish it on anyone.'

'But you came back.'

Trent stares past Jonah. 'I can't change what happened but I can try to fix it. I can change. I had to. It was either that or the drugs would've killed me. I figured facing my shame was better than dying or moving away from home forever. But it's hard. People haven't forgiven me, that's for sure. The whole town hates me.'

'Carly doesn't hate you,' Jonah says.

'No. She's why I came back.' Trent looks at the floor. 'She probably saved my life.'

Jonah doesn't know what to say. He never hated Trent, but he certainly wanted nothing to do with him and would've done anything to keep him away from Carly. He stood beside his mum while she publicly humiliated Trent's mother. Jonah's behaviour was bullshit. He's the one who should feel ashamed and he knows it.

'Man, I . . .' Jonah hesitates. Should he tell Trent about what his mum said? Maybe he already knows. 'I'm sorry, I was . . .' Jonah stops himself and thrusts his hand forward instead, holding it out for Trent. 'You have two people standing with you now,' he says. 'I'm standing with you too.'

Trent looks at Jonah's hand and pauses before planting his firmly against it. They shake.

'Thanks, man. It means a lot. Even if you have a dodgy ankle.' Trent smiles at Jonah. 'But now you gotta go and stand with Beth.'

'Yeah, I do. I have to. Can you apologise on my behalf? To your mum? She's going to be really pissed off.'

'Can I give you a lift back to the Millers?'

'You'd do that?'

'I can't let Carly's little brother go back out there without making sure he's safe, can I?'

'They have guns. It's dangerous.'

'All the more reason to go together.'

Jonah places his strapped foot into his shoe and does it up tight. He takes a deep breath then stands. 'Thanks, Trent. Okay. Let's do this.'

Trent goes to the kitchen to grab his keys, then they head out the door.

TWENTY-THREE
BETH

Dad wakes me. I remember where I am and why and sit up in fright.

'What is it?' I whisper.

'Mum. Her breathing's getting worse. Nothing I can do is helping. She needs a doctor.' The light of a torch picks up the whites of Dad's eyes. His fear terrifies me.

Mum is beside me, propped up on pillows against the wall. She takes tiny fast breaths, her chest moving up and down with the excruciating effort. Her lips are blue.

'What's happening?'

'I'm not sure. The broken ribs might have damaged her lungs,' Dad says. 'I'm going for help.'

Dad takes his gun from his holster, opens the chamber and checks the rounds. He takes out his speed loader and checks that too. 'I'm only taking one gun so I can move faster. Grab me some more speed loaders.'

I do as he says. I fill a bumbag and bring it back to him. Dad straps it around his belt. He kneels down and kisses the top of Mum's head. 'I'll be back with the cavalry.'

Mum smiles. She goes to say something but her words don't come. Fear of losing her balloons in my chest and tightens my throat. I swallow hard.

'Is there anything I can do?' My voice cracks.

Mum shakes her head.

Dad finishes arming himself and squeezes my shoulder on his way past. 'I'll be back,' he says.

I hear him go up the ladder.

'What the . . .?'

I stand and walk around the containers to see what's wrong. A small trickle of water leaks down the wall and is pooling on the ground. Dad is at the top of the ladder pushing up against the trapdoor but it doesn't budge. My heart skips a beat as it dawns on me. The trapdoor isn't opening because the dam is full of water. We went over the bank last night instead of through the pipe.

'The stop . . .' Dad says.

'I put it back after I left last night to find you. I definitely put it back.' My voice sounds panicky.

'Who was last to leave?'

I pause as I realise what's happened. 'Jonah.'

Water steadily flows into the bunker through the trapdoor and air vents.

'They're trying to flush us out,' Dad says. 'They might have found him.'

'What do we do?' I ask. My heart is pounding in my chest.

Dad pushes against the trapdoor one last time then climbs back down the ladder.

'Come with me,' he says.

I follow him into the second storage container. Dad throws me a life jacket and then takes one to Mum.

'It's going to be okay,' he says. 'The bunker will fill with water but the trapdoor is slightly lower than the ceiling, so there will be air pockets. This will give us some time. Once it fills to the right level, we'll be able to open the trapdoor and swim up.'

Dad's calmness starts to rub off on me. My heart slows, my mind stops racing and I start to think methodically.

Dad kneels down next to Mum, moves a strand of hair from her face and tucks it behind her ear. Then he rests his forehead against hers.

'I love you,' he says.

A tear trickles from Mum's eye and runs down her cheek. Then I realise Dad is crying too. I step closer to take a better look. Mum is so pale, her lips blue. She's panting quick shallow breaths.

I move in and kneel beside her.

'We're getting you out of here now,' I say. 'We're getting help.'

Mum looks at me and her hand flails to find mine. Our fingers intertwine. Her eyes fill with tears again but she doesn't close them or look away. The pulse on the side of her neck is throbbing fast. She squeezes my hand. It feels like a surrender, a message. A final gesture.

No.

Mum closes her eyes. Tears stream from them.

'No,' I say. I look to Dad. 'Do something. Please do something!'

'She suddenly went downhill,' he says. 'I was watching her. I thought she was okay, but I should have gone for an ambulance hours ago. We need this thing to fill up faster. We need to get her out now.'

TWENTY-FOUR
JONAH

'I wouldn't go any further than this,' Jonah says. 'I reckon if I head towards the house through those trees then into the channels from there I'll be able to make it. They were holding Lucy in an old stable on the neighbour's place further along. Thankfully they're away on holidays.'

'Are you sure Beth rescued her? From guys with guns?'

'Yep, I'm sure it was them who ran past me in the channel. I got out and hid because I wasn't sure at first, but it had to be. When I made it to the stable some of the men were still there, shouting. A machine had been driven straight through the stable wall.'

Trent smiles. 'Girl's got guts.'

'Yeah.'

'Well, look at her parents. Fuck. She was always gonna turn out that way, wasn't she?' Trent says. 'She'd take on anyone.'

Jonah laughs. Then he takes in a deep breath to try to calm his nerves.

'Right. This is me.' He turns to Trent and holds out his hand again. 'Thanks, Trent. I get what you mean about having someone standing with you now. You coming this far with me has just about given me enough courage to actually do this.'

Trent looks at Jonah's hand. 'I'm not just leaving you out here on your own. Jesus, what kind of person do you think I am? The ol' girl'd kick my arse.'

'Trent, these guys are ruthless. If they catch us I don't know what they'll do.'

'They'd better not catch us then.' Trent grins.

Jonah shakes his head. 'Trent, I can't let you come. If you get hurt or killed I'd never forgive myself. I'm already injured. My ankle feels much better now that it's strapped, but still, I can't move very fast. I don't know what might happen.'

'And if *you* get killed, I'd never forgive *myself*. I don't want to live with that either. I can't.' Trent holds his gaze and this time it's Jonah who looks away first.

'Okay, fine. We can't just sit here arguing. If we're going to go, we have to go now.'

Trent pulls off the road and hides the car behind an old tank. He knows this place better than Jonah.

'See those trees,' Jonah says. 'That's where we're headed. They can hide us almost to the front door of the house. We'll have to run around the back, but we can check whether the white van is there first. Hopefully it's not. Then there's a channel on the other side of the house which we'll run along to the bunker.'

'Right. I'll follow you.'

'If we get separated, run back to your ute and wait near the road. Keep out of sight until the police come. When they arrive flag them down and bring them to the bunker. To get there you need to follow the channel down the fence line until you reach another paddock, go through the gate and you'll see a dry dam on the left. The bunker is at the bottom of that dam.'

'Okay. I know the one.'

Jonah and Trent make their way through the trees. Jonah is slow and clumsy, but they keep going. They use the hand signals Bear taught them at survival camp to communicate. At the time, Jonah thought it was just a bit of fun learning the signals. He never thought he'd ever be using them for real.

Jonah makes it to the house first. He flattens himself against the wall and waits for Trent to dash across the yard. The house seems quiet and there's no van parked outside.

'We're in luck,' Jonah says. 'Okay, so the feeder channel runs along that side of the house.' Jonah points towards the dam. 'If we use the channel we'll have cover all the way to the bunker.'

'That's genius,' Trent says.

'Wait 'til you see the bunker. It'll blow your mind.'

'Let me help you,' Trent says. He stands next to Jonah so Jonah can put his arm around his shoulder. Together they move away from the house towards the channel. Just when they're about to go over the edge, they pull up sharply. They stare into the channel. Jonah is speechless.

It's full of water.

'They must have opened up the turkey nest,' Trent says.

'Fuck!' No longer worrying about their cover, Jonah limps towards the gate and starts running up the road towards the dam. Trent jogs along beside him.

'What is it?' Trent asks.

'When I left I didn't put the stop in the pipe, the one that goes into the dam. If water is down this far, it will also be running into the dam.'

They reach the dam. It's half full.

Jonah swears again. Louder this time.

They stand there for a moment looking at the moonlight reflecting on the surface of the water.

'You think they're down there?' Trent asks.

'They are if they made it back to the bunker last night.'

'I don't get it,' Trent says.

'There's a trapdoor at the bottom of the dam, leading into a concrete bunker. The pipe that goes from the channel into this dam has a stop inside it to prevent the dam from flooding. I didn't put it in and I was the last to leave.' Jonah points further along the channel. 'There was another stop in the channel, just up there, but that must have been pulled too.'

Jonah tries to think clearly. Maybe it's not his fault. Wouldn't Beth and Lucy have come in again that way too? Maybe they wanted to fill the dam, but then maybe not. It was dark when they were running back. They probably went straight over the bank of the dam to save time and didn't see the stop.

'Okay. So what do we do now?' says Trent.

'I'm going in.'

Jonah takes off his shirt and gingerly steps out of his shoes, then he dives into the black water and disappears. He swims straight to the bottom. He tries not to kick with his sprained ankle but every time it moves a sharp pain shoots up his leg. Hopefully the freezing water will numb it soon.

There's no light. All Jonah can feel is mud, no weeds. He's in the wrong spot. He goes back to the surface and sucks in a few deep breaths as he positions himself in the middle of the dam. When he ducks down again, he feels the weeds and runs his hands along the bottom of the dam until he finds the handle of the trapdoor. He tries to lift it but it doesn't budge. He places both feet on the ground and pulls at the trapdoor with all his might. It's as heavy as concrete. When he thinks his lungs will burst, he swims to the surface.

Trent calls to him. 'Jonah, what are you doing?'

'Mate, the trapdoor won't budge.' Panic rises in Jonah's voice as he talks. 'I need a jack. Can you run and get one?'

'Are you *sure* they're down there?'

'I don't know! But if they are they'll drown. It could already be filling with water.'

'What if it's watertight and they're safe? We could drown them by opening it.'

'But what if it's not? If it fills while they're inside and they can't open the trap they'll die. We've got to open it.'

'So you need a jack? Anything else?'

'Scuba gear?' Jonah knows it's a long shot.

'Sorry, mate, can't help you there.'

Jonah gets out of the water and sits on the bank of the dam while he waits for Trent. He dries himself on his shirt and then drapes it over his shoulders to try to keep the wind off. He's freezing.

At the sound of an engine approaching he scrambles awkwardly back down the bank and lies just above the lip of the water. He watches. The vehicle has no headlights on. In the moonlight Jonah can see that it's Trent's ute, but he can't see who's behind the wheel. Awful thoughts of Trent being caught and the men now travelling in his ute flit around Jonah's mind. The car turns and comes straight towards him. Jonah's heart thumps hard. If he needs to he can lower himself back into the water and move away across the dam.

Then he notices his shirt and shoes sitting on the bank. He wants to grab them but it's too late. The car is too close. Jonah lowers himself into the water, leaving only his face out so he can breathe. How could he be so stupid? If they look over at the dam they'll see his shoes.

Please be Trent, please be Trent, please be Trent . . . The words play over in Jonah's mind. Will the men put two and two together and realise the bunker is underneath the dam?

'Jonah,' Trent whispers. 'Jonah, where are you?'

Jonah exhales with relief and stands up in the water.

'You brought your ute?'

'I didn't know how much time we had. I thought it was urgent.'

Jonah limps over to help Trent with the jack and lever. He places the lever in the right place and winds it to make sure it works.

'Don't suppose you have a tyre jemmy?'

'Of course I do,' says Trent with mock offence.

Jonah can hear the smile in his voice.

Trent strips off and joins Jonah in the water. He gasps at the cold.

'We need to tread out to the middle and then duck dive straight down,' Jonah says.

'It's so cold it hurts.' Trent's voice is shaking.

'You'll get used to it. Deep breaths.'

They both dive headfirst into the pitch black. They can't see each other so they have to work by touch. Jonah feels around for Trent but gets nothing. He moves along the bottom of the dam until he finds the trapdoor. He tries opening it again, but it won't budge. When his lungs are screaming for oxygen he kicks his way back up to the top. His head breaks the surface of the water and he sucks in the air.

'Jesus, man, I thought you must have drowned you were down there for so long.'

'We're going to have to do this together,' says Jonah. 'You still got the jack?'

'Yeah. It weighs a ton though. I went down like a lump of concrete and couldn't find anything but mud. It's so creepy. You sure they're here?'

'Like I said, I don't know. But if they are we have to get them out. Okay, this time take heaps of quick breaths first. Hyperventilate yourself. Then we hold hands and go together.'

They both breathe as fast and as deep as they can.

'Okay,' says Jonah. 'Now.'

He takes Trent's hand. They both direct themselves towards the bottom of the dam and kick hard.

Jonah feels his way along until he finds the trapdoor. He places the jemmy under the lip and Trent helps him to wrench it up. Immediately water starts being sucked down into the bunker. Jonah realises that if they open the door all the way, they'll be sucked in too. They'll have to open it just a crack at first and let the water run in slowly.

He wedges the jemmy in, leaving a three-centimetre gap, and they kick up to the surface.

'I really hope we're doing the right thing,' Jonah says as he gasps for air.

'Me too,' says Trent. 'We can only try.'

'If they are safe down there, we're flooding them out right now.' Jonah shakes his head.

'At least they can get out now. But what if Bear thinks we're them? The guys after them?'

'I didn't think of that,' Jonah murmurs. 'They're not going to be able to see it's us until they're out. Even if they have a flashlight, the water is too muddy.'

'All we can do is keep ducking down, wait at the trapdoor and help them through it when the levels equalise,' Trent says. 'And just pray Bear doesn't kill us when he comes out.'

'Or Beth,' Jonah says.

'You ready to go back down?'

'No, but let's do it.'

They hold hands and duck dive straight down, swimming among the weeds until they feel the draw of the water. Jonah pushes the jemmy further into the hinge, opening the trapdoor wider. They kick back to the surface.

'How long will it take?' Trent asks. 'How big is the bunker?'

'It's as big as the dam,' says Jonah.

TWENTY-FIVE
BETH

A gush of water grabs my attention. Dad and I look up. My heart gallops. We run to the trapdoor and see an iron bar wedging it open.

'They're here,' I say. 'They're coming for us.'

Dad disappears into the storage container and comes out armed to the hilt. He carries an inflatable mattress and battery operated pump. He starts it up and within a few minutes the mattress is full of air. He lifts Mum onto it, then sits her up and places a life vest over her head and secures the straps. He props her up in a sitting position with pillows.

'Beth, while it's filling, you stay with Mum. There are handles on the sides of the inflatable mattress. The main lights will go out soon, but the orange emergency light will stay on.' He places a helmet with night vision goggles on my head. 'This will pick up heat even through water. We'll rise to the surface together with Mum.'

Dad continues to give directions like we're on one of his survival camps. Emotionless, methodical, professional. I notice a slight American accent creeping into his speech now too. Everything seems like a dream, only the pain and fear in my heart is too real.

'I'll exit first and deal with any threats. Then you and Mum go straight up to the surface. Mum's not going to be able to swim, so it's up to you to get her to the top.'

'What do we do once we're out?'

'We do whatever it takes to get Mum to hospital.'

Mum makes an inaudible noise. Her lips form a word. She is trying to say something.

'Leave me,' she mouths.

'No.' I look away because I don't want to see those words. I don't want to consider what they mean. 'No,' I say again.

The gushing gets louder as the men above us wedge the iron bar closer to the hinge, opening the trapdoor a little further. They'll be waiting for us outside. Will they shoot us? We'll be sitting ducks.

I realise I'm no different to Carlos. Hatred burns inside me like an inferno. If I get the chance to kill them I won't hesitate. I'll be glad they're dead.

The lights flicker and extinguish. I pull down my night vision glasses and hold onto Mum's mattress.

My entire body is shaking. I don't know if it's from fear, anger, the cold or a mixture of all three. As the water rises we float up with it, me on one side, Dad on the other.

Dad keeps talking, telling us what to do once the bunker fills. I'll have to move Mum off the raft, then pull her down into the water before we can exit through the trapdoor. Our vests will want to float, so it won't be easy. Once we're through, I'll get Mum out of the water, we'll deal with whatever we have to deal with, then we'll get help. Things are going to be okay.

Dad's words are calming and bring the reassurance and comfort I need. The panic in my throat remains, but it isn't escalating like it was.

The rise feels slow even though a huge volume of water is gushing in. I'm cold, but Dad says my body can handle it. We'll be fine. I keep moving my legs, keep pumping my blood.

When my head's almost touching the ceiling, the noise of the water rushing in finally stops. Silence. It feels like we're in the eye of the storm. Using my night vision, I can see Mum on the inflatable bed, motionless. My heart races at the sight of her limp body. It can't be too late. I reach out for her hand and squeeze it, but there's no response from her. I place my hand in front of her mouth. I'm sure I feel something. I'm sure the air moved.

'Beth, it's time. We've got to go. You right?' Dad says.

'Yes,' I say. 'Go.'

I watch Dad's dark form bob down under the water. He pulls himself down the roofline towards the trapdoor and then disappears through.

After a moment I follow. I pull Mum down but we keep bobbing back up to the surface. I fumble with my lifejacket and remove it. I take a few deep breaths and then, with all of my strength, kick down. Mum bobs up and hits the edge of the trapdoor. Her jacket snags. I push her through and let go. She disappears, rising up at rocket speed. I follow. Up, up, up – my lungs about to burst.

My head breaks through the surface. I suck in a huge breath of air. There's yelling. Desperate voices. Names. On the bank of the dam Dad is on top of someone, gun to his head.

'Don't shoot! Don't shoot! It's Jonah and Trent Granger.'

Confusion dissipates as we realise we are not under attack. Dad drops his gun.

'Get Lucy,' he yells.

Dad and Jonah dive back into the dam and drag her out. Panic takes over my body. I kick and splash my way to the edge and scramble out after them. Dad has his back to me and is blocking my view. He is bent over Mum, attending to her. It's not until he places both hands together and pumps on her chest that I realise what he's doing.

Jonah is on his knees beside Mum.

'Do compressions. I'll count,' Dad says to Jonah.

In the distance, blue and red flashing lights come into view. Trent runs to his ute. He takes off, wheels spinning. The tail end of his ute whips around, his lights go on and then he floors it towards the gate.

Dad and Jonah talk in broken sentences to each other.

'Now. Increase speed. That's enough. Wait.'

Dad leans down and breathes into Mum's mouth.

'It's tight. Like it's blocked.'

Trent's lights reach the end of our driveway and he turns around, leading the police convoy back towards us. I stand up, panic rising as I watch Mum's lifeless body. I want to run towards them, tell them to hurry up. Trent pulls up first, then a police car and ambulance. There's lights, boots rushing back and forth, bags dropping on the ground and radio static. I'm pushed out of the way as they focus on Mum. Dad and Jonah are told to step back and the paramedics take over.

Things are happening so fast. Mum is carefully moved, her clothes cut, her body dried. Packets are opened and discarded. Airways, IVs, chest pads. Counting. Drugs. Confirmations of dosages. Disjointed words. Fluid actions . . .

No response from Mum.

No crack of hope in anyone's voice. Just numbers, doses, voltage. A man yelling 'Clear'. Jolting.

The shrill noise of flat line.

No response.

'Keep going with the compressions,' someone says. 'We can't shock asystole.'

More compressions. Adrenaline.

Drugs go into the IV, compressions are counted. A man squeezes a balloon connected to a tube going down Mum's throat.

'The oxygen won't go in.'

'It may be a pneumothorax,' says a paramedic.

They keep going, keep pumping. A large needle goes into her chest. There's a hiss of air escaping.

'Yep. Definitely a pneumothorax.'

They keep working, gloved fingers moving fast, trying to bring Mum back to life. I lose track of time. I just sit helplessly on the bank, a hard ball of despair choking my throat. This can't be happening.

'Shall we call it?'

Wait . . . what's happening? What does that mean? I stand up and shuffle towards them.

'How long have we been going?'

'About forty minutes now.'

Wait. Does *call it* mean stop? They can't. They have to keep trying. While they are trying there's hope.

One paramedic nods to the other.

'No. No. Don't call it. Please don't call it,' I plead with them. 'Please.' The words rush out of me.

The paramedics look my way.

'I'm really sorry,' one of them says. He takes my arm and tries to lead me away.

'No. No. No,' I cry. It's the only word I can form. It repeats in my head long after I stop saying it. A sob rises in me. I pull my arm away and scramble forward. 'Please,' I say. 'Please.'

I kneel by Mum's chest and continue the compressions. Tears pour from my eyes and fall onto her. 'Please, help us,' I say. 'Somebody, please.'

The paramedic puts his arm around my shoulder. 'C'mon,' he says gently.

'No,' I scream. 'No. No.' I fall onto Mum's chest. Sobbing. 'Come back. Come back.'

Behind me there's a noise. It starts slow and guttural, almost inhuman. I turn to see Dad fall to his knees. He arches his back to the sky and lets go of the loudest, most violent roar.

Police are startled. No one moves.

Dad falls forward and crawls a few paces on his hands and knees. Deep sobs escape from him. An officer starts towards him. Another officer reaches out to stop their colleague.

'Leave him.'

Everyone turns away or looks to the ground, not knowing what to do.

I turn back to Mum's lifeless form. A paramedic places a blanket over her. I pull it right up to her neck.

The paramedics sit back on their haunches, eyes still lowered to the ground.

I lift my eyes and scan around me. The lights are dizzying, everything's in slow motion. Jonah is sitting on the ground, wet and shaking, his head in his hands. His raspy breath staggers in and out of his chest. Indecipherable words crackle from a radio. The water in the dam is like black glass, motionless and cold.

I turn back to Dad, but the bank is empty. He's gone.

A blanket goes around my shoulders and I'm guided to the back seat of a police car.

Lights and faces.

Words that don't make sense.

A weird numbness moves into me. I don't feel like I'm there anymore. My mind rises up, away from everything happening on the ground. Out of reach. Safe.

The darkness of the night envelops me and enters my soul, cold and hateful. Someone starts the car and puts the heater on then leaves me alone. My crying is uncontrollable. Something that keeps happening whether I want it to or not. Like the water flowing in the channel, like the world spinning, like my heart beating. I want everything to stop and I hate that it hasn't. Every beat of my heart is one more second since Mum's heart stopped.

Police keep checking on me but eventually they leave me alone and I'm glad. I just want to sit here, tightly wrapped in my blanket, cocooned in the darkness.

Cars come and go, people mill around. All the vehicles move slowly now, like they are sad. Lights dimmed, engines idle. Voices have quietened.

A few men in suits huddle together and look towards where I'm sitting. I look around for Dad. Where is he? Why isn't he here?

My need for him explodes in my chest. It's sudden and impactful and a cry comes from inside me. I can't stop it. I open the car door.

'Dad?' I cry. 'Dad?'

One of the men in suits rushes over to me.

'Where's Dad?' I ask.

'Hey, hey. It's okay. We'll find your dad,' he soothes.

Find him? What does he mean?

'Where is he?'

The man puts his arm around my shoulder like he has nothing else to say.

'Where is he?' I ask again. I look to the other men. 'Where's my dad?'

'Is there someone we can call for you? A family member? Someone who can sit with you?'

'No,' I mutter. 'I haven't got any family.' Saying these words out loud is like being punched in the gut. Mum is my family and she's gone. Dad is my family and he's missing. Sobs rise inside me and escape with every breath.

Mum is gone.

It doesn't seem possible.

'What about a friend?' the man asks gently.

I look at the person talking to me. I don't know what he's talking about. I've lost track of the conversation.

I just want to see Dad.

'Where's Dad?' I ask again.

'We don't know where he is, Beth. But we're going to find him.'

The words start to sink in and images of Dad on his knees, screaming into the sky, flash through my mind. His grief, raw and protesting. His fury.

Oh no.

'He's gone for them,' I whisper.

'Who?'

'Carlos. The men. The men who came for us. Dad's gone for them.' Nerves tighten my stomach. There are four of them. All armed with guns.

TWENTY-SIX
JONAH

The police won't let Jonah talk to Beth. He wants to tell her he's been here the whole time. He wants to tell her that he didn't leave her, that he followed her to help rescue Lucy. He wants to tell her that he loves her.

'Beth,' Jonah calls.

She doesn't turn around. She's motionless. A silhouette in the headlights.

A policeman guides Jonah to another car. 'Please, I need to talk to Beth,' Jonah says.

'It's best you don't. For the investigation. We need to get your statement first.'

Jonah stops walking and looks at the cop.

'I'm taking you back to town. You can see Beth after giving your statement.'

Jonah hesitates. Everything feels wrong. Lucy dying, not being there for Beth, Trent being taken away, Bear disappearing. But if this means he's helping then he'll do it. It just feels wrong. He wants to hold Beth, tell her that everything is going to be okay. But is it? Since yesterday everything has turned to shit. How is that possible?

Jonah sits in the back of the police car with his head leaning against the window. He looks out at the blackness, as deep and as vast as space. The ride back to Deni feels like forever. When he gets there, the police station is as chaotic as it was at the farm. Police dart back and forth, getting ready to take statements. The station is cramped and over-crowded. An officer walks out of an interview room and leaves the door wide open. Jonah can see Trent inside, sitting behind a desk with a polystyrene cup in front of him. Trent's mum is in another room with a detective, their door also wide open. Carol talks through heavy sobs.

'I told them to wait until I got back with the police,' she says. 'They could have been killed.' She looks up and sees Jonah. 'My son could have been killed,' she repeats, staring straight into his eyes. The detective glances over his shoulder, then springs up and closes the door.

Police move Jonah along the corridor and open the door to an empty interview room.

'Grab a seat in here and keep that leg up. I'll be back in a minute.' The officer closes the door and leaves.

Jonah sits down and stares at the wall. He's confused about what's happening. Why can't he talk to Beth? He assumes the police need to question everyone separately first, to get the full story. That must be what's going on here. He'll sit patiently and do as they say. He'll do whatever it takes to help Beth.

TWENTY-SEVEN
BETH

I turn off the interior light and open the car door a crack so I can hear what's going on. Mum is completely covered now and the commotion around the dam continues. Police are debating whether or not there really is a bunker beneath the dam. They talk about getting divers, then they discuss finding a pump to drain it. I could tell them what they need to know, but I stay put.

They're still arguing when an unmarked car pulls up and a woman steps out.

I recognise the woman as Tania Carter, Deni's local detective. Carter takes control and immediately defuses the heat.

'Has Beth been questioned? Is there a team ready to go after Bear?'

The officers mumble their responses and Carter walks back to her car to get an ETA on the chopper. Then she turns and walks towards me.

'Hi, Beth? I'm so sorry. Can I ask you some questions?'

'Yes,' I say.

'I don't know everything that's happened yet, but I know you've been through a huge ordeal. We have a special team of police coming but I need your help so we can look after you and your dad now.'

'He's gone after them,' I say.

'Your dad?'

'Yes. I'm sure of it. There's things . . . We're not . . . Dad knows them. It's personal. He was an agent in America. I don't know which agency, I only found out yesterday.'

Carter looks confused.

'We moved here in witness protection,' I explain. 'When I was nine months old.'

Carter stalls, but then recovers her words. She walks around to the other side of the car and gets in to sit down beside me. I look out the window, hoping to see Dad coming back. A glimmer of light sits on the eastern horizon and the water in the dam is a dull grey. I divert my gaze away from where Mum lies on the bank. It still doesn't seem real. Tears sting my eyes.

Carter closes her door.

'Can you tell me everything you know? From the beginning?' She listens intently while I tell her the full story, leaving nothing out.

'. . . and then Dad just screamed. It kind of scared everyone so much they stopped what they were doing. Then they all quickly looked away, like they wanted to give him privacy. I was with Mum. I don't know how much time passed, but when I looked for him again he was gone. I'm scared . . .' My voice drops away but I push through it. 'I'm scared they'll kill him.'

'The police on the scene, what did they do?'

'Everything got so crazy. I was screaming for Mum, Jonah was calling for me, the police were trying to calm things down, the ambos were ordering the police around . . .'

Carter wraps her hand around mine. 'We're going to find your dad, okay?'

More vehicles pull up and police in black uniforms arrive. I don't recognise them. They must be the guys from Sydney that Mum called. The extraction team. They seem to take over the scene as soon as they arrive, like they're the most important people there.

'We could put the drone up to have a look,' I say, suddenly remembering. 'I know where they were before.'

'You have a drone?'

'Yes. It was in my pack. I dumped it out here to help Dad get Mum into the bunker.'

We step out of the idling car. The police have already found the bag with the drone. Carter instructs them to bring it to me.

I place it down on the ground and turn it on. It whirs to life. Everyone watches. The drone goes straight up and I move it forward. Once the drone is out of sight everyone diverts their gaze to the monitor. The early morning light is dim, but we can make out the channels, roads and rice bays.

Then the white van comes into view. It's stark against the dark landscape. It's on its side, half in, half out of one of the channels. My heart leaps at the sight of it. I zoom down so the drone can see in the window. There's a man inside, behind the driver's wheel. A rifle lies across his lap. His head is resting on a strange angle, his eyes open but vacant. Dead.

'Jesus,' says one of the men in black. 'We have another crime scene. Where is that?'

I point in the general direction as I steer the drone higher into the sky.

'There,' says one of the police officers.

He points to something on the screen. A black mass among clumps of weeds in one of the rice bays. I zoom the drone in closer and then lower it down. It's a man lying on the ground, facedown. I know it's not Dad because he has hair. Dad's head is shaved. I breathe a sigh of relief.

The police start to discuss who will be in charge of what at which scene. One officer suggests the entire farm and neighbouring properties be made a crime scene.

My fingers tremble as I manoeuvre the drone back up into the sky. My need to find Dad bubbles inside me like boiling water. I can't stand it. The drone is high in the sky, following the road back to Clive's old machinery shed.

There's nothing else of interest until we get onto the Youngs' property. I fly the drone slowly over the machinery shed and stable. Then I see it. Another man down. I zoom in closer. This man is easily visible because he is in the clearing out the front of the shed. He's holding an M16 rifle. My heart pounds like a jackhammer as I bring the drone down. Movement diverts my attention to the left of the screen. It's Dad. I can tell instantly by his size. But then I see something that makes my blood run cold. The man with white hair from the stable is creeping around the back of the shed. He has Dad in his sight and looks like he's going to shoot. Dad's moving in the opposite direction and can't see him. I shove the drone's control panel at the nearest officer and sprint to the police car that I was sitting in. Carter yells at me as I dash past her. I jump into the driver's seat, put the car into drive and plant my foot. The wheels spin as the back of the car slides out. Police officers scream at me, some getting out of my way, others running towards me. I pull onto the track that goes through the paddock towards the Youngs' place and gun it.

When I reach the end of the road I pull up in a cloud of dust. I slam the gear stick into park and get out. I have a channel to cross. It's empty but I jump it anyway, landing on the opposite bank without slowing my pace. I run towards the machinery shed where I saw the white-haired man.

I can hear them well before I see them. They're fighting. The sounds of fists on flesh, boots connecting with torsos and grunting through gritted teeth come from inside the stable. I pump my legs harder and run with no idea of what I'll do when I get there.

When I reach the back wall, where I drove the digger through, my whole body is thrumming, adrenaline coursing through my veins.

There's more punching and the sound of a body slamming against the tin wall. Then everything stops.

What happened? My heart lurches at the thought of it being Dad injured, or worse.

I creep along the damaged wall until they come into view.

The white-haired man is holding his gun to Dad's head. Dad's rifle is on the ground a few metres away. The man steps back, keeping his revolver on Dad as he kicks the rifle further away. I reach down to my ankle and unclip my knife from its holster.

'You've come for me, Carlos, and here I am. So what are you waiting for?' Dad says.

'Where are my men?' snarls Carlos.

'They picked the wrong morning to try and kill me. There're a dozen cops just over the paddock there,' Dad says. 'You're not getting out of this.'

'You think I care about getting away?' Carlos laughs. 'You and your good-for-nothing brother took everything from me. Finding you and your worthless family is the only thing that's kept me going. Once I kill you, I don't care what happens to me.'

Dad has a brother?

'What are you waiting for then? I'm here. Do it,' Dad taunts.

'There's a certain order.' Carlos sounds smug.

Pressed against the wall, I stay out of sight. My heart is racing. I can see Dad. He looks relaxed, defiant. The side of his face is smeared with blood.

'This is where your grand plan isn't so grand, Carlos.' Dad smiles. 'Even if she was here, you wouldn't get the satisfaction of making me watch my child die. She's not mine. I'm not her father. She's my brother's, and I held him while he died at your place seventeen years ago.'

Carlos hesitates.

'Liar,' he roars.

'It's true, she's not mine. All you've done today is make her an orphan.'

As my brain processes these words, everything slows. I brace against the wall to steady myself as I sway. An ugly sob rises to my throat and escapes. Dad's eyes flick towards me. Carlos turns.

'Beth?' says Dad.

I step forward. I go to speak, but I don't know what to say. My grip around the knife is loose. I shuffle it into a comfortable hold as my eyes meet Dad's. My jaw clenches as I search his face for the truth. Truth about him, truth about me. Was he lying? Playing some kind of bluff? I can't read his expression.

My eyes move to Carlos's hand, still holding the gun at Dad's head. I focus, whip my knife up and release it with all the force I can muster. It spins across the room, a silver flash, and lands on target. Blood spurts out of Carlos's wrist and the firearm clatters onto the cement.

Dad moves like lightning. He swings his fist at Carlos and delivers a punch to the face. He follows through with a series of kicks and punches until Carlos staggers across the floor and hits the wall, knocking over a cluster of jerry cans. Dad makes a dash for the gun. He raises it towards Carlos. I brace myself for the explosive bang, but it doesn't come. Dad lowers the firearm as unleaded petrol glugs out of a jerry can in front of him. The fuel pools across the floor.

Carlos sits with his back against the wall. He reaches into his pocket and pulls out a silver lighter.

He holds it over the fuel with an orange flicker and a threatening, self-assured smile.

Carlos grabs another jerry can, unscrews the lid and pushes it over. Petrol sprays out as it falls and then settles into a rhythmic, pulsing stream, slowly spreading across the room.

Carlos gets to his feet.

'Think about it, Carlos . . .'

'Oh, I have,' Carlos interrupts. 'I've had a lot of time to think.'

Carlos moves closer to the doorway.

'There's police everywhere,' Dad warns. 'You'll never get away.'

Carlos smiles and releases his grip. The lighter twists as it falls. There's a puff of an explosion as the liquid ignites. Orange flame tracks across the floor, alive and merciless. Dad runs towards me.

'Go!' he screams. I turn and dive back through the ripped wall. The stable explodes like a fireball as I leap through the air and land on the ground outside. Dad follows and lands beside me as flames lick up the walls and spread across the roof. In seconds it's a roaring inferno. Thick black smoke fills the roof space and plumes out of the building, rising high into the sky.

Dad and I get to our feet, shielding our faces and moving back from the intense heat of the flames. It's alarming to see how quickly the fire takes hold, how quickly it went from the lighter dropping from

Carlos's hand to the building being fully ablaze. Police cars pull up on the other side of the channel and officers start running towards us. I want to yell that they should be running around the other side of the building but my voice is hoarse.

Dad turns to me, gives me a look I don't understand and then raises his hands to show he's unarmed, almost like he's surrendering. I don't know if he's in trouble, but I can certainly see that he doesn't want to be perceived as a threat.

I can tell he wants to say something to me, but police swamp us, their numbers multiplying by the second. They separate us, escorting us to different cars. Dad keeps turning to me.

'We'll talk about this, Beth,' he says. 'We'll talk. I'll explain everything.'

My breath catches in my throat. He doesn't say, 'It isn't true. I'm your father.' He says, 'We'll talk about this.'

I stare at him. The shock silences my thoughts, my feelings, my words. I'm blank. Numb.

I'm led to a car and sat in the back. The door closes. I stare out. Dad's words ring through my head.

All you've done today is make her an orphan.

All you've done today is make her an orphan.

All you've done today is make her an orphan.

TWENTY-EIGHT
JONAH

Jonah sits in the interview room and waits for his mum to arrive. Ida goes to bed early so she wouldn't have known Jonah wasn't home until the police called. Jonah's never done anything like this before. He cringes at the thought of how angry she'll be.

Jonah rests his ankle on another chair, leans his head back against the wall and closes his eyes. He sees the image of Lucy on the bank of the dam, Beth sobbing onto her chest and Bear screaming into the night. He opens his eyes and tries to think about something else but can't. It's all-consuming and leaves no space in his brain.

The door opens and Ida rushes in like her presence will save Jonah's life. Her brows are knitted together, her mouth a thin straight line. She gasps at the sight of Jonah's swollen eye, then she notices his bandaged ankle.

'Oh my God,' she says.

'I'll give you two a minute,' says the police-woman. 'Mrs Keath, would you like tea or coffee?'

'No, thank you,' Ida says shortly. She's snappy, but it's because she's mad at Jonah, not the officer.

The door shuts.

'What have you got to say for yourself?' Ida says.

Jonah's tears come thick and fast now that she is here.

Ida stands firm, arms crossed in front of her. Jonah can see she's ropeable for being called down to the police station at the crack of dawn and for that text Jonah sent her last night. She already knows he lied about where he was and what he was doing, but she obviously has no idea what's happened.

Jonah blubbers, unable to get his words out. 'Beth's mum . . . Lucy . . . she's dead.'

Ida's jaw drops, her whole demeanour changing in an instant. 'What? How?'

Jonah tells Ida a rushed and disjointed version of the events. Then he puts his head down on the table. 'Lucy died because of me. She came to save *me*. If it wasn't for her it'd be me who was dead.'

Ida goes into overdrive with questions and she's suddenly very concerned about Jonah's ankle and the cut above his eye.

The police officer comes back in. She fills Ida in on a few more details of the story then takes Jonah's statement. When they're finished Jonah is taken to another room where his injuries are photographed. The police offer to take him to the hospital but Jonah refuses, he just wants to be alone.

'I'll make sure he's seen to,' says Ida.

When Jonah's released he's exhausted. Ida insists on taking him to the hospital where his cut is seen to and his ankle is X-rayed. Nothing is broken, but a nurse straps it properly for him. He is given crutches and told to stay off it for a couple of weeks. Finally he can go home. He sits in the passenger seat of his mum's car and stares out the window. How did things get so messed up? His heart breaks for Beth. He wants to be able to hold her, to bring her comfort.

Jonah thinks back to when he first really noticed her. When he started falling in love with her – or maybe it was when he first admitted to himself he was already in love. It was at Jonah's first comp two years ago. Beth had been sitting opposite Jonah, cross-legged on the mat. She was one person in a circle of ten, and her smile lifted her face. Her back was straight and her hands rested on her knees. Her toenails, a fluorescent pink, stood out against the stark white of her karate uniform, pressed to perfection.

'My name is Elizabeth Miller and I'm from Deni . . .'

At first Jonah had stopped to listen because she'd called herself Elizabeth. It sounded strange. She'd only ever been known as Beth at school.

Maybe that was what made Jonah tune in and see her differently. Her confidence. He noticed how smooth and mellow her voice was. It was something he wanted to hear more of, something he could have listened to forever. She kept talking, telling the others about herself. Jonah's gaze fell on her lips; moving, gleaming, perfectly shaped. He wondered what they would feel like pressed against his. Then she smiled. She was done talking and that smile lit something inside Jonah that has never been extinguished since. The next person introduced themselves, but Jonah's eyes were still on Elizabeth Miller.

A long silence had brought Jonah back to the room. Everyone was staring at him. He realised it was his turn to speak.

'My name is Jonah Keath and I'm also from Deni,' he said quickly. He went on, but he was distracted by Beth's eyes lingering on his chest, then moving up to his face and meeting his. Was she really doing that or was he imagining it? Either way, Beth was a wild distraction. Jonah finished his spiel and the next person started to introduce themselves.

Beth glanced at Jonah, her dark eyes twinkling, before she looked to the girl talking.

Suddenly, Beth's politeness was the most attractive thing in the world. Those who think kindness isn't hot haven't met Beth. Physically, she was gorgeous. Smokin'. But so are lots of girls. Beth was so much more than that. The best thing about her was *her*. She not only knew, but also truly liked who she was. And when Jonah was with her, he liked who he was too. Beth's quiet confidence made Jonah's heart race and his voice catch in his throat. From that day, Jonah's eyes were always on Elizabeth Miller. When she walked with him across the oval after school, at the lockers, in the canteen, in the street. It's like he'd never seen her clearly before that day, and suddenly he couldn't stop seeing her.

Bear would have throttled Jonah if he could have read his mind that day. Jonah remembers Bear's gaze moving around the gymnasium and lingering on him – or was Jonah just imagining it? Bear terrified Jonah, still does. He scares the crap out of all the guys in town, even though deep down they wish they were just like him. And now Jonah wanted nothing else than to date his daughter.

Did Bear know then? Has he always known?

Even before yesterday Jonah was never sure one day to the next. He was waiting for it though. The guys at school told Jonah he was out of his mind, that he must've had a death wish. He didn't. His love for Beth had just outgrown his fear of Bear.

But none of that matters now. Everything has changed. Who knew the difference between heaven and hell was twenty-four hours?

Even if Jonah and Beth still love each other, their relationship is doomed. Jonah played as much a part in Lucy's death as the man who pulled the trigger. He led those men to the Millers. It was his fault they were found after seventeen years of hiding. Because of him, Lucy died. Because of him, Beth lost her mother, her identity and her life as she knew it.

Jonah knows that it will be a wedge between them. Something that can never be removed. It can't be explained away or retracted, and its magnitude is too big for a mere apology. Jonah finally understands what Trent said about regret – never being able to run away from it and it eating your soul. Jonah gets it now. It's well and truly inside him. He can already feel it.

Ida slows down as they turn into their gate. The driveway is about two hundred metres up to the house and Warra is walking along it, just ahead of them. He's wearing dark jeans and a black coat with his hands jammed in the pockets.

Ida pulls up and presses the window button.

'Hi, Warra, jump in. We can give you a lift the rest of the way.'

'Actually, I'll get out here,' Jonah says, opening his door. 'I need some air.'

'Your foot, Jonah . . .'

Jonah pauses. 'I'm okay, Mum. I'll use the crutches.'

Ida drives the rest of the way and parks around the back of the house.

'Hey,' Warra says. 'I heard what happened.'

Jonah looks across the paddock. 'News travels fast,' he says. 'At least your bike survived the ordeal unscathed. It's at the police station ready to be picked up.'

'I wasn't worried about my bike. I came out to see how you were.'

'Thanks, man, but shouldn't you be at school?'

'I took a mental health day.' Warra smiles.

'Six kays is a long way to walk. I appreciate you coming.' Jonah's voice cracks.

'Nah, I got a lift with my uncle. He's having a look at your neighbour's field bin across the road so he let me out at the gate. We're on our way to the Websters' place to see about doing some work for them.'

They walk on in silence, Jonah wobbling on his crutches. When they reach the gate Warra walks towards the old shearing shed rather than the house. He takes a seat on the platform. Jonah sits down beside him.

'So how are you doing?' Warra asks.

'Bit sore,' says Jonah, gesturing to his foot.

'I don't mean that,' Warra says. 'I mean how are you feeling?' He taps his chest. 'Here.'

Jonah shakes his head. His eyes flush again and he tries to hold back the tears. He doesn't want to cry in front of Warra, but his eyes leak like a dripping tap and the tears spill down his face one after another. Jonah can't find his voice.

'I heard they got you after Bear. They tied you up and shit.'

Jonah touches the red marks on his wrists where the zip ties were.

'That's totally fucked. I'm glad Bear killed them all.'

They go quiet again.

'It's my fault, Warra. All of it. Did you hear that too?'

Warra looks Jonah in the eye. 'No,' he says firmly. 'No one's saying that.'

'Well, it's true,' Jonah says. 'You know that photo I put up on Instagram? When I won the championship? Bear was fist-pumping the air in the background.'

'I'm not on Instagram,' says Warra. 'What's that got to do with anything?'

'Bear had these rules. Beth told me to take it down but I didn't. Then the International Fight Organisation shared it. Whoever those guys were, looking for the Millers, that's where they saw it. I may as well have written their address in the fucking sky.'

'I think Instagram is heaps more effective than skywriting.' Warra smiles. 'If you'd written it in the sky out here only about five people would have seen it, and they would have already known the Millers' address.' Jonah looks at Warra and his smile fades. 'Sorry,' he says.

Jonah smiles weakly, only for a second. He appreciates Warra's effort to lighten the mood, but the sadness comes in relentless waves.

'Anyway,' Jonah continues, 'I blew their cover. Their seventeen-year cover. And Lucy died because of it, because of me.'

'You can't say that. It wasn't because of you, it was because of whatever happened years ago back in America. That's why Lucy died. Shit like that catches up with you. If not now, tomorrow. If not tomorrow, next week or next year.'

'You don't get it.' Jonah's voice is tight.

'No, I do. I do get it. More than anyone, I fucking get it, Jonah.'

Something in Warra changes, like he's bracing himself. Jonah stays quiet.

'Years ago we all used to hang out down at Guya Bend. My cousins, uncles and aunts . . . There were heaps of us. One day I was in the river, playing in the water. I'd been told not to go out too far or the current would take me. We were throwing a frisbee, and I was jumping and diving to catch it. Then I must've dived the wrong way. I put my feet down and the ground wasn't there anymore. I couldn't swim. I dog paddled like fuck to stay up but I was going nowhere against the current and tired out fast. The other kids started screaming to everyone on the bank. They came running. I paddled and paddled and tried to keep myself up to breathe but I took in a lot of water. I could hear splashing and yelling but I couldn't turn around to look. I couldn't see if anyone was coming for me. I went under. I hit the river bed, so I kicked and kicked and thought it was over because I couldn't direct myself back up to the surface. The current pulling me back down was too strong. Then I hit something. A branch. I was just about out of breath, but I grabbed onto it and clawed my way along, one hand in front of the other until my head broke through the surface. I stayed there and held on for dear life. The branch was so thin I thought it would break. If it did I knew I was a goner. I tried to stay as still as possible, not wanting to jerk the branch around. I could still hear my family yelling. At first I thought they couldn't see where I was, then I realised they were yelling for my uncle.'

Warra takes a sharp breath. 'He'd dived in to save me. He could swim, but he had an old shoulder injury from football. I'm not sure if that's why he never came back up. I guess no one will ever know.'

Jonah looks at the ground. He's stunned. 'I'm so sorry, Warra. I never knew that story,' he says. 'Why didn't you tell me?'

'I only ever talk about it with one person. My other uncle. He told me there is never a single event that leads to an accident. Events before an accident start way back, but it's always the last thing that happens that gets the most blame.'

Jonah sees what Warra is saying.

'He said guilt would make me sick, like a disease. Instead, he told me that I had to live a life my uncle, his brother, would be proud of.'

'You're doing it, Warra.' Jonah smiles. 'You're the wisest person in the whole school. Your uncle would be real proud.'

'I hope so, but I'll never *know* that either. I changed that day. I've never been the same. That will happen to you.'

'I can feel the change,' Jonah says. 'I just don't want it.'

'Yeah,' Warra says. 'I didn't want it either.'

They look out over the wheat field.

'Thanks for skipping school and coming out here, mate.'

Warra shrugs. 'I doubt there'll be much happening today anyway. Beth's friends are all crying, they're really worried about her. The story is getting more warped each time it's told. People aren't sure what's true anymore.'

Jonah thinks of when Trent got into trouble with the police. The stories flew around town like wildfire, changing and growing with every new breath.

'I can imagine,' he says.

This story will be a part of Jonah now. When he's talked about, or introduced, it will wheedle its way into the conversation to help explain who he is. In Deni, everyone has a tagline.

Warra pushes himself off the platform and onto his feet as a ute slowly makes it down the driveway.

'That's my uncle, gotta go.'

'Thanks for dropping by,' Jonah says.

After Warra goes Jonah stays seated on the platform, gazing out over the farm. He lies down and elevates his foot like the doctor told him to. Now that it's properly strapped it feels much better. He thinks about Warra's story. Jonah can't believe that he's known Warra since prep and yet Warra's never told him the real story behind his uncle's drowning. Jonah doesn't really remember it. Like Warra, he would've only been nine. For a town where everyone thinks they know everything about everyone, it sure holds a lot of secrets. People really know jack shit about each other. Like all of Jonah's thoughts, this one leads back to Beth. Beth didn't even know her real name. What a terrible way to find out the truth.

Jonah edges off the platform and uses his crutches to make his way back to the house. Ida and Carly are sitting at the kitchen table. They hush when Jonah shuffles in.

'What?'

'We were just talking about you,' Carly says.

'Nice,' Jonah snaps.

'We're worried about you, you jerk,' Carly shoots back.

Jonah stops walking. He's sorry but he doesn't want to say it. 'You heard from Trent yet?'

Ida clucks her tongue but Jonah ignores her.

Carly shakes her head. 'No.' Her tone is sad.

'You will,' Jonah says. 'We talked about you.' Jonah turns to his mum. 'He's not the person you think he is. He's clean for a start, and he's a good guy. He helped me. He didn't think twice about it, even though it was dangerous. The town needs to give him a second chance. You need to give him a chance.'

'Jonah, I don't dislike Trent. I just don't want him dating my daughter,' says Ida. 'There's a difference.'

Jonah ignores her and looks at Carly. 'And you're right. I'm a jerk. I was a jerk when Trent got into trouble and I was being a jerk just now. I'm sorry.'

Carly smiles wide. 'Cool, I'll forgive you if you promise to keep working on de-jerking yourself.' She giggles. 'That didn't come out right, did it? Eww, bad visual.'

Jonah laughs. With a loud sigh, Ida gets up and leaves the room. Jonah goes to his bedroom to lie down. He's totally wrecked but sleep doesn't come. He wonders if Beth is still at the police station. He needs to see her.

His eyes drift to his bike helmet on top of the bookshelf. Without any more thought he's up, off the bed with the helmet in his hands and heading out the door.

Carly runs after him. 'Where are you going?'

'Police station. If Beth isn't already there she will be soon.' Jonah stops. 'I'm going to ride. Do you want to come?'

'Is Mum letting you go?'

'Probably not.' Jonah shrugs. 'I'm not asking. I need to be there for Beth.'

'You're on crutches.'

'I'll leave them here.'

Carly stares at him.

'Trent might be there,' Jonah says.

Carly smiles. 'I'll drive,' she says, grabbing the keys to the ute.

TWENTY-NINE
BETH

Detective Carter sits in the back of the car with me. We're still waiting to leave the farm.

'Who's with Mum?' I ask.

'A couple of the local guys,' she says. 'She will be conveyed into town soon. To the . . . hospital.'

She means morgue but doesn't want to use the word. Same thing though. The morgue is at the hospital. I have to keep reminding myself she is gone. Every time I think about it I feel this overwhelming dread. It hits my heart, my chest, my stomach. And then there's me. My life without her . . . I can't get my head around it.

Dad's in a separate car. I have no idea what will happen to him. Will he be charged? Did he really kill those men, or was it self-defence? As for me, I stole a police car. At least I didn't drive it on a public road, so they can't charge me for that. And what about Carlos? Have the police gone after him? Is he still out there?

As thoughts crash around my mind, a helicopter comes into view. It's searching. He's still out there.

Firetrucks arrive and make their way towards the blaze. Clive will be shocked when he finds his stable burned to the ground. Then I shake my head. What am I thinking? That's nothing compared to finding out your neighbours of seventeen years are ex-agents hiding out. Farmers can cope with a fire just fine.

I breathe in . . . I breathe out.

My problems stay with me.

Air goes in . . . air goes out.

My heart keeps beating. The world keeps spinning. Life rolls on.

Only the world inside me has stopped.

A policewoman finally gets into the driver's seat and we start moving. We pause at the front gate of our property to give way to the undertaker's van that pulls out in front of us. We follow it into town. If I turn my head I can catch glimpses of Dad in the car behind us. We pass the police station and turn the corner to the morgue. Neither our driver nor Carter tries to make small talk and I appreciate it. I need this time. My eyes rest on the rear window of the van. Mum is right there in front of me. Out of reach forever. Shot at close range three times by a high-powered rifle. Rage sears my insides. I'm glad those men are dead.

Life doesn't seem possible without her. I think of the kids at school who have lost a parent. There aren't heaps, but definitely some. When I was in year eight a guy at school lost his mother just before the mid-year holidays. He took that week off. Then when we all returned three weeks later he was back. His life rolled on. I told him I was sorry, but it was for my benefit. I did it because I felt I had to break the ice and say something. I couldn't just cruise into the term like nothing had happened. Now I realise the size of the hole blown right through the middle of that guy's heart.

Numbness, detachment, confusion, disbelief and bouts of fury. White-fiery hatred.

We pull up in the car park and the van reverses in. A door opens and two hospital orderlies step out. Dad and I wait with two officers standing between us. The world feels warped; motions are slowed, sounds are amplified and my vision is too sharp. The rear door of the van is opened and Mum is brought out and transferred to a hospital stretcher. She is completely covered. I'm not sure how I'm supposed to act, so I just stand there and stare. It's like it's not my mother, like it's not even a person. The orderlies indicate for us to follow. They wheel Mum while Dad and I walk behind her. No one says a word. There's only the sound of the wheels rolling on the squeaky-clean laminated floor.

We reach two large doors and go through. The orderlies stop. A man has a form on a clipboard. Dad steps forward, takes the pen and writes something. This is it. This is goodbye. Again, I'm not sure what to do. I edge closer to the stretcher and reach out. My fingers tremble as they hover just above her. I pull my hand away.

'It's okay,' the man says. 'You can say goodbye.'

My face crumples at the sound of the word goodbye. I step forward and lean down to hug her. I can feel her shoulder through the canvas and I know it's her. I place my head against the sheet.

'She's so cold,' is all I can say. She wouldn't like that. She hates being cold.

Loud sobs escape me as I rest my head against hers. I hold her tight, never wanting to let go.

'I love you,' I whisper. 'Thanks for being my mum.'

When I release her I step back and turn, not sure what to do next. I'm not allowed to talk to Dad, and police are watching us closely, but then he's there, arms open, hugging me, and we cry together.

———————

I'm escorted back to the police car and driven around the corner to the station. When we pull up out the front, I see Willow, Jonah, Trent and

Carly waiting on the steps. It's overwhelming, but I appreciate that they're here. It breaks the ice about Mum — it works both ways.

'Have you heard everything?' I ask Willow as she throws her arms around my neck.

'I've heard a lot of things, some of it too crazy to believe so I'm waiting to hear it from you.' Her chin starts to quiver. 'I heard about your mum. I'm so sorry.' She can't hold in her tears. I hug her and we cry together.

'Thanks for being here,' I say.

'Of course,' says Willow.

Carter stands close, ready to intervene if we start talking about the case.

'I'll tell you everything after I make my statement,' I say.

'There are so many stories flying around. Is it true you're all from a Russian intelligence agency?' Willow asks.

'No. That's not true at all. Where did you hear that?'

'At school this morning.' Willow smiles through her tears. 'So I'm guessing you weren't genetically modified and bred as an enhanced fighting machine either?'

Even in the darkest of moments Willow can make me smile.

Jonah stands back. I finally look his way. He looks exhausted. The cut above his eye has some medical gauze over it but I can see that the bruising and swelling is still coming up. He only has one shoe on, the other foot is strapped in a tight bandage. The chemistry between us is awkward and strained. A mix of anger and grief prickles my skin. I want to hug him and scream at him all at once. I'm relieved he's okay, but I need time to work out how I feel. To sift through everything that's happened and what it means.

The hug option is the least confronting, so I go with that.

Carter steps in. 'Sorry, no contact between witnesses,' she says.

I look at Jonah. 'We'll talk.'

Jonah chokes up as Carter ushers me into the station. 'I'll wait for you,' he calls.

'We're all waiting for you here,' Willow says. 'And you're welcome to stay at my place until you're ready to go home.'

I turn to look back. My gaze locks on Jonah. Behind him, Trent is standing next to Carly. Jonah and Trent came back for us when they didn't have to. I barely know Trent, yet he risked his life for me.

'I know you guys came back to save us,' I blurt out, needing to tell them. 'You dived into that freezing water and . . . did what you did to open the trapdoor and get us out. Thank you. If Mum was here she would want to thank you too.' My voice cracks. No one speaks because if they do, their tears

will spill over. Sometimes crying can be suspended –
a delicate meniscus held intact by silence.

I turn and go inside.

A support person arrives and then the question-
ing begins. I go over every minute detail, leaving
nothing out. The whole process takes hours. They
offer to give me a break for lunch but I pass. I want
to get this over with. I'm informed that there is a
full-scale search for Carlos underway, but so far
they haven't found him. Police have been to Rams
Oval and retrieved our phones. They're going to
examine them and then decide if I get mine back.
I tell them I want to speak to Dad.

We're given an interview room for privacy. His
exhaustion gives him a wild, haunted look.

'What's going to happen to you?' I ask.

'What do you mean?'

'With the police . . . are you in trouble? Those
men . . .'

'No, no, Beth. I'm not in trouble.' Dad shifts his
weight in his seat. 'I knew Carlos would still be at
Clive's stable, so I went to find him. I wanted to
arrest him but I knew the local guys would have
to wait for a special team to arrive before they could
go in. I didn't want to wait. I knew we didn't have
much time. Backup would have been useful, but
explaining it to the police at the scene would have

taken too long and they would never have let me go. I knew once the police arrived he'd run, that he'd try to get away and come for us again later. He needs to be put back in jail, Beth. When I came across his men they were still looking for you. They had guns and weren't going to come in quietly. It was me or them. I had to defend myself.'

'Have you killed people before?' I ask. 'In America?

Dad doesn't answer.

'How many?'

Dad frowns. 'Beth, what are you thinking?'

'I don't know! I don't know what to think. How am I supposed to be?' My tone is accusing but I can't help it.

'There are no expectations.'

'How should I feel about you?'

Dad looks at me.

'So you're my uncle,' I say, holding back tears. 'The operative who died was my father, your brother.'

'I've known you since the day you were born. I've been with you every day since you were nine months old. I've raised you as my daughter. I love you as my daughter.'

'The love for a niece is different to the love for your own child, though, isn't it?'

'Never doubt my love for you, Beth.'

'My whole life has been a lie — lies you fed me. And now you ask me not to doubt you?'

Dad stays quiet.

'I don't even know who you are,' I say.

'It's only my past you don't know about. You know who I am.'

I shake my head. 'How does this work now? How did it work after my . . . your brother died? You and Mum, it's weird. Were you really together? Or was it all a charade?'

Dad glances at the door.

'Tyler, your biological father, my little brother, died in my arms.' Dad pauses to maintain his composure. 'I told him to hold on, that the ambulance was on the way, but he knew. He knew he was going. Your mum was there too. He told her to take you away and keep you safe. Then he looked at me. He asked me to promise to look after you, to protect you. I promised.'

I feel like I've been dropped on my head and my brain has shattered into fragments. I'm trying to process it all but nothing is clear, nothing is defined. I have questions, but I'm not sure I can handle the answers.

I look away from him.

'You should have told me we were in witness protection.' My eyes come back to his, accusing.

'We had it covered.'

'No. Clearly you didn't,' I snap. 'I had a right to know.'

'We did what we thought was best.'

'Well, you were wrong. And that's rubbish! You didn't tell me because you didn't trust me.' My anger spills over like a pot on the boil. I try to pull it back but it spills again. I can't stop it because the fire burns blue-hot beneath it. I realise I'm yelling. 'I had a right to know *before* I was running for my life in a channel, *before* my boyfriend rode into a death trap and *before* Mum got shot! If you'd told me, things would have been different. Mum might still be alive.'

'Beth,' Dad soothes.

'My name is Kennedy,' I snap as I stand. I go to leave, but then stop. 'What do we do now? Where's Carlos? Will he come after us here in town?'

'I don't know, but it's very likely. We don't know where he is.' Dad clasps his hands together. 'We've arranged for a couple of guards to watch you. They'll go everywhere you go, they'll protect you, but I'd rather you stayed here and waited for me. When I finish up we can go home. I know you're hurt and angry and I'm sorry, but we have to work through this together.'

I shake my head and pause. 'I can't go home. Not yet. I need time and I need space from you. I'm going to stay at Willow's tonight.'

'Beth! It was all to protect you,' Dad says as I walk to the door.

'Don't call me that! That name is a lie. My whole life is a lie. Even you! You're not even my father.'

My voice becomes shrill. I rein it back to a fierce whisper. 'I had a right to know!'

'Beth, don't you walk through that door.'

I wrench it open and a group of police jump back, pretending they weren't listening.

'Beth!' Dad booms as his frustration reaches its peak.

I storm down the hall towards the door. Carter is waiting for me.

'Whoa, hold on, Beth. Before you go we need to discuss a few things,' she says.

She takes me into her office. 'Take a seat and try to calm down.'

I glare at her.

'It's fine for you to leave, but you're going to have a couple of guards following you around. Carlos hasn't been caught yet. I recommended you be put into hiding but Bear said you'd refuse. So, until Carlos is found, this is what's happening.'

'Yeah, Dad just told me.'

'Okay then, I'll walk you out and introduce you.'

I follow Carter back to the entrance. Willow, Jonah, Trent and Carly are still sitting on the front steps of the police station. They spring up when they see me coming.

'You okay?' Willow asks.

I don't answer.

Two men step forward and flank Carter. I assume they're my security.

'This is Tim Lee and Stewart Riggs. They'll try not to be intrusive, but they will go everywhere you go until further notice.'

I shake hands with them and say hello. They must be from the city. They're both dressed in black suits that look completely out of place in this town. After the introductions, Carter bids us farewell and makes her way back into the station.

I turn to Tim and Stewart. 'I'm going to go to Dad's karate gym to get some clothes from my locker, then I'm heading to Willow's place.' I rattle off both addresses. I should be terrified, but the thought of Carlos coming after me again is just exhausting. All I want is to go to Willow's place and lock myself in her room, away from the world.

Tim hands me a card.

'Both of our names and numbers are there,' he says.

'Thanks,' I say. 'And thanks for what you're doing. I'll feel much safer knowing you're there.'

I realise that's not exactly true. I'd feel safer if Carlos was in jail. Or dead. The truth is I don't know how I should be feeling. It's like nothing is sinking in. I guess it's too soon to know what is or isn't broken inside me. I'm all mixed up and mashed together. It will take a while to sift through and decipher what's what.

Willow's fingers curling around my arm brings me back to the present.

'This is . . .' She searches for the right word. 'Unbelievable.' Willow looks up at the two men standing in front of us. 'Do we just walk and you follow? Do you walk with us? I mean, how does this work?'

Stewart smiles. 'We can give you a lift if you'd like. If you'd rather walk, just try to forget we're there. We'll be following in a car. When you go into the gym, one of us will be at the front door, the other will go around the back to check entry and exit points. We'll wait for you to do whatever you're doing, then we'll give you a lift or follow you to the next place. You go inside and after we check things out, we sit outside.'

'All night?' asks Willow.

'If Beth is inside your place all night, then yes. That's where we'll be.'

I can see Willow is already forgetting that a killer is out there and is romanticising about having her own bodyguards when she's a famous actor.

'But Carlos is fifty kays away, isn't he?' I say. 'Aren't they still searching for him out at the farm?'

Stewart pauses, like there's something he wanted to avoid telling me. 'A tractor was stolen from a paddock near the location Carlos escaped from. It was found eight kays away in the Frankels' machinery shed. A ute was missing but found soon after on the side of the road in a parking bay. There were other tyre marks next to it, like a car had been parked there. If that's the case, and he's taken it, the owners don't know it's gone yet as no one's reported a missing car.'

I check the time. It's been hours and the police have no idea where Carlos is. He could have easily made it into town by now.

Willow must realise the same thing because she tightens her grip around my arm.

Carlos could be anywhere. Waiting.

THIRTY
JONAH

Jonah can't read whether Beth wants him there or not. She talks to him, but she is distant, closed off somehow. He knows he can't push it. Beth's always had Willow. They've been inseparable since he can remember. He envies Willow for that. Jonah wishes Beth was going to his place.

Beth has too much on her plate for Jonah to even begin to contemplate how she might be feeling. Working through their relationship issues is insignificant compared to everything else that's happened. It could be months before Beth can deal with anything else. All he can do is wait.

And he will. He'd wait forever.

Beth and Willow decide to get a lift to the gym with the police. By the time Jonah and the others arrive, the officers have checked the entry and exit points and cleared it as safe. Bear's gym used to be a furniture shop. In the middle is a large open space covered in mats. Around the edges are punching bags. There's a tiny changing room, bathroom and office at the back. It's pretty basic, but it's only designed for karate training and fighting. There aren't any machines or weights like in a regular gym.

Once they're inside, Carly runs around like a lunatic kicking and punching the air, making stupid noises and pretending she's a ninja. Trent, Jonah and Willow sit and watch her. She doesn't give a shit how silly she looks.

Beth disappears into the change rooms and takes a shower. She always has a change of clothes here. Willow offered some of hers, but there's no way Beth would fit into Willow's clothes. Beth is a giant next to her.

Jonah checks the clock a few times. Beth's been in there for ages.

'Do you think she's all right?' he asks.

'Maybe not, but she's not going to be all right for a while, is she?' Willow says sadly. 'I doubt anything has really sunk in yet. Knowing Beth, she won't fall apart with everyone around, so we should give her some space. All we can do is make sure we're nearby when she needs us.'

Willow's probably right, but Jonah can't help but feel useless and a little resentful that Beth's going to Willow's house, not his. Jonah can't change what's happened, but he wants to be able to help Beth. He wants time alone with her so they can talk. He wants her to know he's there for her. And most of all, he wants Beth to forgive him so he can one day forgive himself.

Although his guilt is heavy, deep down Jonah knows that Warra's right. None of what happened is solely his fault. A whole heap of things led to last night, and many other people had a hand in it: Bear, Lucy, Carlos, of course, plus anyone else who was involved in whatever happened all those years ago. They left unfinished business and now it's caught up with them. It's unfair that Jonah has to feel guilty. Could he have known that posting a picture on Instagram would lead to the exposure of a seventeen-year witness protection cover? Or someone's death? Nevertheless, Jonah can't deny that he played a part, and maybe he'll never be able to forgive himself for that. The only innocent one in all of this is Beth. The question is whether she can forgive him.

Carly has stopped fighting thin air and is quiet. She sits down by Trent and they lie head to head, looking at the ceiling and talking. Trent runs his fingers through Carly's pink hair and every now and then she giggles. They're lucky. Their relationship is simple. Sure, Jonah's parents are an obstacle, but they're outside of the Carly-Trent bubble. There is no wedge between them. That's how he and Beth were yesterday, in their own perfect bubble. Jonah can't help but think about what happens when a bubble bursts. The soapy film holding it together disappears into the air and leaves no evidence that it ever existed. The thought depresses him. Will he and Beth stay together? Or will their relationship disappear into thin air too?

Beth finally emerges wearing faded denim jeans and a black T-shirt. Jonah thinks she looks best like this. Natural. Amazing. Her hair is damp and hangs loose down her back, wetting her T-shirt. As she walks she scoops it up, twists it into a bun and fixes it to the top of her head.

'I think all the energy I had left just went down the plug hole,' Beth says. 'I could have stayed in there forever.'

'Well, when we get to my place you can climb into bed and go straight to sleep if you want,' suggests Willow.

'Sleep is exactly what I want.' Beth sighs. 'I want to go to sleep and stay asleep.'

Jonah can't think of the right thing to say so he keeps quiet. He knows he's not invited to Willow's so, for now, this is goodbye for him. He's not going to get time alone with Beth. There will be no time for words, for tears to fall, for hugs. That's what he wants more than anything else, but he doesn't want to push her. He knows she's exhausted. They both need to sleep.

'If you want, you're welcome to stay at our place too,' says Jonah. Carly shoots him a look. He has no idea if what he said is true. Who knows, maybe their parents will demonise the Millers like they did Trent and the Grangers.

'Thanks,' says Beth. 'I'll see how things go.'

A silence follows. Everyone is unsure of what to do.

'Okay.' Willow breaks the silence. 'We may as well get your bodyguards to drive us, yeah?'

Beth nods. Her eyes flick to Jonah and then away again.

Beth picks up an overnight bag and throws it over her shoulder. Jonah stands. As Beth passes him she stops.

'Bye,' she says. She puts her free arm around his neck and pulls him close. Jonah wraps his arms around her as Beth kisses him hard on the mouth. His eyes close and his heart melts. The kiss is over as quickly as it started, but the sensation of Beth's lips on his lingers long after.

Carly and Trent hang back as Jonah walks Beth and Willow to the car. When they drive away, it's like all of Jonah's energy goes with them. He aches with emotional and physical fatigue.

'I think I want to go home,' he says.

Carly's eyes linger on Trent's. 'I'll meet you later.'

'Yeah, look, you guys do what you've got to do.' Trent walks to Jonah's side. 'You okay?' he asks.

Jonah nods but doesn't say anything, he stares straight ahead. Trent raises his eyebrows at Carly like he doesn't know what to do.

'Okay, let's go,' Carly says.

Jonah gets into the ute and waits while Carly says goodbye to Trent. He winds down the window and feels the cool breeze against his face. His arms and legs are heavy. He moves his gaze slowly to take in his surroundings. The rows of bare trees, the flat grey sky, the sound of birds being drowned out by a truck going past. He thinks of Beth curling up in bed, her eyes closing, her heart aching. He still feels that kiss and wonders if it was their last.

THIRTY-ONE
BETH

'You climb into bed and I'll bring in some food,' Willow says.

I walk through the house and straight to her bedroom. Willow's room is large with a queen bed that we share. My parents are strict, but they let me stay here whenever I want, and Willow is always welcome at our house.

I realise that I'm still thinking of Mum in the present tense. It doesn't feel real that she's gone. I have to keep reminding myself it happened, that it wasn't a nightmare. She is actually gone.

Willow comes in with a cheese toastie and hot Milo. This is my favourite comfort food at Willow's place. I love that meals don't focus on protein here. I can eat whatever I want regardless of carbs and fats. They even have a jar in their pantry full of mixed lollies that I dive into whenever I'm over.

I take off my watch and put it on the bedside table next to a photo frame resting facedown. I pick it up. It's a photo of Willow and Sam. I'd forgotten she was going to break up with him. I haven't even asked her about it.

'I'm so sorry,' I say. 'How'd it go?'

Willow glances at the picture. 'Oh, it's done. We're both sad. Him more than me, though, and I feel awful about that – but please, this doesn't even rate compared to what's happened to you in the past twenty-four hours. I mean, everything seems like a big deal until something really important happens. Then it's put into perspective.'

Something about what Willow just said doesn't feel right. 'You can't be like that,' I say. 'It is important. How you feel is important to me. I'm sad about you and Sam too.'

Willow's eyes well up. She shakes her head. 'There are too many sad things right now.'

I take off my jeans, climb into bed and pull up the covers. Willow climbs in too and lies on her side to face me.

'I'll stay here until you go to sleep,' she says. 'If I'm not here when you wake up I'll be in the house somewhere.'

'I'm not scared,' I say, but it's a lie. I'm terrified. I'm scared to think about what my life is now, to figure out who I am, to live without Mum. I'm scared of what life will be like with Dad, my uncle. What is he to me now? I'm scared of being without him, of being an orphan. Most of all I'm scared of being Kennedy Jane when I was happy being Beth Miller. As much as I want to push Kennedy away and stay Beth, I feel compelled to search for my truth. I feel compelled to be her.

'Really?' Willow's eyes widen. 'Aren't you worried that that guy is still out there somewhere?'

'I probably should be, but I don't feel threatened this very minute. There's just so much else to think about.'

Willow's eyes well up again. 'I'm so sorry about your mum.' Tears stream down her face. 'Lucy was like a second mum to me. I'm going to miss her so much.'

I nod and roll onto my back to stare at the ceiling. A numbness fills my chest, making me feel strange and detached inside.

'Dad's not my real dad.'

'What?' Willow dabs at her eyes.

I turn to her. 'Bear's my uncle.'

Willow stares at me.

'My biological father was killed during the police operation that put us into witness protection. Dad placed himself with Mum to help raise me because it was his brother's dying wish.'

Willow is silent for a while.

'Sorry . . . It's just . . .' She brings her hand to her head, spreads her fingers and makes an explosion noise. 'Mind. Blown.'

'Mmm, mine too.'

'I don't even know what to say.'

'Me neither.' I turn my gaze back to the ceiling. 'I'm going to be Kennedy,' I say.

'Won't that be weird?'

'Totally,' I say.

Willow exhales a laugh. I laugh too. It's a short but welcome relief.

'Kennedy Jane,' Willow says. 'I like it. You could be a stunt woman with that name.'

'What if you don't like her?' I ask.

'Well, if she says mean things or kicks puppies I won't like her. But if she's anything like Beth Miller, I think I'll like her just fine.'

I laugh again.

'But seriously,' Willow says. 'How will Kennedy Jane be different to Elizabeth Miller?'

I don't answer. I need to hold that question up to the light and examine it myself. Will she be different? And if so, how and why?

'I'm not the same person I was yesterday,' I whisper.

'Yeah, but even if you were still Beth you wouldn't be the same person you were yesterday.'

'True,' I say. 'It hurts my brain thinking about it.'

I close my eyes and it feels so good I leave them closed. The darkness seeps into my brain and eventually I sleep.

———————

When I wake it's dark. For a moment I'm confused and then I realise where I am and why. Everything rushes back and just about winds me.

Mum is gone. My tears rise up and flow out of me like rivers. I yearn for her, for Jonah and for Dad too . . . I yearn for them and yet I hate them. All of them. I yearn for my life two days ago. Ignorance *was* bliss. But now I know the truth and I'm shattered. I blame them. Mum and Dad, even Jonah. I try not to, but deep inside I resent him for the part he played in us being found. It's a bitter pill.

But we can't turn back time. We can't fix these mistakes. It's final, etched in stone. The damage can't be undone. My heart pounds in protest and frustration, in rage. Sobs rise inside me and release but the pressure doesn't change. My pain is all consuming: physical, mental, emotional. How will I do this? How do I go on with this raging inside me?

The darkness folds around me and I'm thankful for it. The soft, rhythmic sound of Willow breathing in bed beside me brings me some comfort. She's always there, as sure and as constant as the sun rising.

I roll my shoulders, trying to open my lungs. I hate the restriction I'm feeling, the tightness in my chest that has moved in like bad weather refusing to lift. Willow rolls onto her side. Her breathing is no longer slow and deep. I stay still, hoping I don't wake her.

'Kennedy, are you awake?'

My stomach lurches at the sound of that name. My real name. It's the first time I've been called by it.

'Yeah,' I whisper.

'Do I really call you that? It feels so weird.'

'So weird.'

'Are you okay?'

'No. I don't think so.'

'Can I help?'

'You are just by being here.'

'Always,' Willow says.

'Are you okay about Sam?' It's obvious I'm diverting the conversation away from myself, but Willow allows it.

'I think I feel relieved. He's really nice and a lot of fun, but something was missing. That magic you and Jonah have . . . When I saw that I realised Sam and I didn't have it.'

I close my eyes at hearing Jonah's name. I'm not sure I can be with him anymore. Not without being reminded of Mum getting shot, of being trapped in the bunker, of kicking through freezing water – my lungs burning, panic rising. Of Mum dying. Of us being found. Our relationship feels heavy and water-logged – dysfunctional, like the bunker. I try to remember him before this, to remember *us*, that magic. It comes to me in patches – disjointed visions and feelings. The tingling of my lips after a kiss, the laughter, my heart racing at his touch, my breathlessness when our eyes met . . .

'What did you see exactly?' I ask.

Willow laughs. 'It was written all over you. The way you said his name, how your lips curled up at the corners when he was near, the flush in your cheeks . . . that last kiss you gave him. I've never kissed Sam like that. Sam's never kissed me like that. I'm sorry to break it to you, but your magic is as blatant as the moon is bright.'

'Is there anyone else? Someone you think about?'

Willow pauses. 'Mmm . . .' she says, like she's thinking.

'I know who it is,' I say, to put her out of her misery.

'You do?'

'Of course. Warra. It's so obvious. He's got it for you too.'

'I think I've always had a crush on him.' Willow sighs. 'Oh my God, those eyes.'

We both giggle and then fall quiet for a moment. 'I'm not sure I can be with Jonah now,' I say, my voice breaking. 'After everything that's happened.'

'Why?' asks Willow, shuffling over to me. 'What's changed?'

'I think I blame him.'

'For what?'

'Everything,' I say.

Willow pauses. I can tell she's thinking of how to say she disagrees with me.

'You don't have to agree,' I say. 'Please treat me the same as you did before Mum died. You can say whatever.'

'I know about the Instagram photo, but how was he to know?'

'I'm not saying he did anything on purpose, but the result was the same. He's the reason we were found.'

'Yeah, and your parents were the reason you were hiding.'

'I blame them too,' I say.

'What should they have done differently?'

'They should have told me.'

'And what would you have done?'

This questions burns in my chest like indigestion. 'I don't know,' I say. More tears flood my face.

Willow puts her arm around me. 'It's going to be hell for a while, but you're going to get through this. You're going to be okay.'

I cry on Willow's shoulder until my tears run dry and my throat is raspy.

We lie in bed together until it's light outside. It's Saturday and Willow's house is bustling with kids getting ready for sport. The mower roars on the front lawn and I can hear Willow's mum, Jodie, yelling at the younger kids about losing their shoes. I love the commotion of Willow's house. The chaos is warm and familiar.

Jodie knocks on the door and enters our room.

'Hey,' she says. 'I'm about to head out but just wanted to check in to see how you're doing?'

'I'm okay,' I say. 'Thanks, Jodie.'

'She's not,' says Willow.

Jodie sits on the side of the bed and squeezes my hand. 'Well, with what you've been through I'm not surprised. You're welcome to stay here whenever, your dad too. He'll be over soon to pick you up.'

'Thanks, Jodie,' I say. 'I really appreciate it.'

'Well, I mean it.' She looks at Willow. 'Dad's around all day today. I don't want you home on your own either with that maniac still on the loose. Bear says they think he's made a run for it, but they're not taking any chances just yet.'

It suddenly hits me what it means for Willow's family to have me here. I'm putting them all at risk. As soon as Jodie goes I sit up. It's time for me to face the day. I should go, and not come back here until Carlos is captured.

'You don't have to get up. You don't have to do anything,' Willow says.

I pull on my jeans. 'If I don't force myself to move I'll spend the rest of my life in here,' I joke.

My head aches from crying. I need to go home, but when I think about going there I feel sick.

'I wonder where Dad is,' I say.

'Mum said he's been working with the police,' Willow says. 'He's got his mobile phone back now. Yours is waiting to be picked up. Someone rang and left a message.'

We move to the kitchen. Willow puts on the kettle and drops four slices of bread into the toaster. While she finds condiments, I peer out the window and see my two guards in a black sedan out the front.

Willow's dad, Frank, comes in from outside. He's kicked his boots off, but his sock guards are covered in grass that's dropping onto the floor as he walks into the kitchen.

'Hi, Beth.' He pats me on the shoulder. 'I'm so sorry about your mum.'

'Thanks, Frank.' I don't know where to look, so I keep watching the car out front.

He follows my gaze. 'There's another car with two more guards in the laneway out the back. They aren't taking any chances.'

'Really?'

'Beth's real name is Kennedy, Dad. Kennedy Jane.'

Frank looks at Willow and nods, understanding the message behind her words. His eyes come back to me. 'Kennedy Jane is a good, strong name. If you decide to use it let me know so I know what to call you.'

I smile. 'Thanks, Frank.'

'So, you have family over in America?' Frank sits down, leaning forward on his elbows.

'Yeah, apparently Mum's and Dad's parents were still there when we left, but I'm still finding everything out.'

Holding back about Dad really being my uncle makes me feel deceitful, but I can't say it to Frank. Not yet. Not when I haven't accepted it myself. The betrayal of the whole thing still cuts like a knife in my heart. It makes me think of a kids' book Mum used to read me called *Who Sank the Boat?* I never believed it was the mouse, not when the other animals were so much bigger. But now I see how it might have been. Finding out that Dad is my uncle is not the biggest or worst thing that has happened to me in the past forty-eight hours, but on top of everything else, it might be what I am struggling with the most. Whoever said the truth will set you free didn't know what they were talking about. The truth will bowl you over and kick you in the teeth. The truth is ruthless.

'Will you go over to meet them?'

The question takes me by surprise. I hadn't thought about this yet. 'Yes, I hope so,' I say. 'But I don't have a passport . . .'

I wonder if my name was changed legally. I have the sudden urge to go down to the police station to speak to someone who might know.

Willow plonks some toast and tea in front of me. I make myself eat even though I'm not hungry. There's a knock at the door and Frank gets up to answer it.

The moment I hear Dad's voice anger prickles my skin. He's here to pick me up. I finish eating and take my plate and cup to the dishwasher. Willow disappears and comes back with my bag. We hug and it makes me want to cry. She is the only thing in my life that is the same as it was yesterday. I squeeze her tight but can't form any words to thank her.

Dad and I haven't spoken yet. Willow and Frank walk us out to the footpath but in a moment we'll be in the car, just the two of us. In the distance I see Jonah hobbling down the street with Warra. I'm not ready for another conversation with him yet either. I pretend I don't see them and get into the car. After waving goodbye to Willow and Frank we drive away. My phone is on the dash in a clear plastic bag. Mum's too. I stare at it, then look away.

'How are you doing?' Dad says.

I shrug because there's no easy answer. Grief comes in waves, my thoughts are spasmodic. There are too many visions, emotions, words and thoughts competing for air time, one shouting over the other. One minute I'm angry about my life being a big farce, then conversations with Jonah play over and over in my head. Next minute I see Mum's face in the moonlight, pale blue and cold. I think about life without her and I can hardly breathe. Then there's questions about my biological father. What was he like? I don't know how I feel about him. My family in America, what are they like? And finally there's life still rolling on – my English essay is due, I need to hand in my maths homework and I'm missing netball training this afternoon.

Meanwhile in my head I keep hearing *I'm an orphan, I'm an orphan.* How did this happen and where did my perfect, happy life go? I hate the bitterness. Then I'm angry about that hate. I feel mean and snarky towards Dad and this hurts us both when we're already hurting enough. I have this awful feeling inside me, one that I can't quite grasp. The feeling of living in lies and betrayal, yet I know there were reasons. It's not rational to feel that way, but try telling a heart what to feel.

'I'm fine,' I say.

We head out of town towards the farm. My stomach churns at the thought of driving onto our property, the place where Mum was shot, where she died. I'm not ready. I'm not sure I can face it, or whether I want to live out there without her. It all seems too far away. Pointless.

Dad doesn't push for conversation. I turn and look out the back window. The other police car is following us.

'How long will those guys be with us?' I ask.

'Until we know where Carlos is. He'll turn up somewhere. He can't hide forever.'

'We hid for seventeen years.'

I pick up my phone and turn it on. My phone beeps as messages come through. The most recent one is from Jonah.

Hey, saw you go past this morning. Hope you're doing okay today. xx

When we pull into our property everything from that night comes back. Mum and I running from the white van, the first time I saw she was carrying her gun, watching Jonah come in this very gate on his bike, Mum being shot. I think of those men standing over her like proud hunters, telling me I'm next. Then everything gets rushed and dark and wet and cold. Endless angst and running and fighting and fire and screaming and crying.

Then it was all too late.

The damage was done.

And here we are, back on the farm, facing the aftermath. We're together but I feel alone. It's not just Mum we lost. We lost ourselves too.

I notice the front door has something wedged in it to keep it shut. The wood is pockmarked with bullet holes that go right through it. I pause on the doorstep and look around the yard. The branch that fell from the old tree when Mum rigged it up as a diversion lies on the lawn, half-tangled on the fence. My gaze rests on the place where Mum fell. When I close my eyes I see the flash from the gun, one, two, three, and Mum jolting with each impact. I turn and go inside.

The house has been dusted for fingerprints. I stand near the spot where Jonah lay and remember how hard my heart was thumping while I untied him. Then we leaped from the veranda and ran for our lives while Mum covered us.

Why didn't I listen and turn right out of the shed? If I'd just turned right like I was supposed to, Mum might have got away.

Tears come but I blink them away.

Dad goes into his room and closes the door. I have questions but they can wait. I go to my bedroom. Time alone allows my thoughts to lengthen and slow down but I'm too restless to stay sitting on my bed. I walk around the house feeling discontented. I go outside and sit on the front step and look at the garden. The garden isn't great, but Mum liked things to be green. My grief both fills and empties me; my heart, my gut, my chest, every limb. I'm filled with an insatiable void.

Another text comes through from Jonah and it feels like pressure, like he wants something from me that I just can't give him right now. I put my phone aside without reading it. This in itself makes me feel bad. I know I shouldn't blame him, but I don't think I can be with him after all this. I can't see him or think of him without thinking of everything else.

My phone rings. I switch it to silent and walk away so I can't see it.

THIRTY-TWO
JONAH

Beth isn't answering her phone and Jonah doesn't know if it's intentional or if she's doing other things. He's sure she saw him in the street outside Willow's place. Ambling down the footpath on crutches, he's hard to miss. The thought burns. Would she ignore his texts too? Maybe she's not at the house. There's no reception out there unless you're close enough for the booster to kick in.

Warra grabs them a table in Little Echidna's Cafe on the main street and they order milkshakes. Jonah sits his phone on the table in front of him and stares at it.

'You all right, dude?' asks Warra, a crease forming between his brows. 'You look like shit.'

Jonah doesn't answer. He just sips his drink.

'You going to school Monday?'

'I guess,' Jonah says.

'What about Beth?'

Jonah looks up and meets Warra's eye. He hates the question. It only reminds him that he has no idea what's going on with Beth, despite the fact they're supposed to be in a relationship. Willow would know, and Jonah hates that even more. 'I don't know,' Jonah says finally. 'I haven't heard. But I doubt it, she'll need some time.'

Jonah's okay with Beth taking time from school, but he's not okay with her taking time from him. He knows it's selfish, but he feels so powerless. Even if she was returning his calls, he can't broach the subject with her yet. You can't press someone who has just lost their mother. He has to give Beth all the time she needs. He knows it, and he'll do it, but it's agony. Sitting around waiting to find out where things stand now is torture. What if Beth needs months? What if she never forgives him? Does she blame him for what happened?

Jonah's never known anyone who has gone through what Beth is going through. This kind of thing only happens to people on the news or in movies. How will the Millers recover from what's happened? Will they even stay in Deni now that their cover is blown? He might never have a moment alone with Beth again. But Jonah can't ask those questions. It's too soon to ask anything.

He just has to be there when Beth is ready to talk. If she's ever ready.

Jonah pushes his milkshake away. He feels sick.

Beth doesn't show up to school on Monday. Kids crowd around Jonah, wanting details about Beth that he doesn't have. No one asks how he is. He was bashed and tied up, he thought he was going to die, but no one seems to care about that.

'Give it a rest,' Jonah snaps.

Willow walks into the canteen and the group leave Jonah to flock around her, hoping to get more info.

'Beth is okay considering what she's been through,' Willow announces. 'Everything else I know has been told to me in confidence, so if you have any other questions you'll have to wait until she's back and ask her yourselves.'

Jonah grits his teeth . . . *Everything else I know has been told to me in confidence* . . . like she's the most important person in Beth's life. Willow looks straight at Jonah and he's sure she looks smug. She walks over to where he's sitting, knowing everyone is watching her.

'Hey, Jonah. How are you doing after everything?' She says it quietly and turns her back on the others so they can't hear.

'I'm fine,' he says, before grabbing his crutches and shuffling away.

He's not going to confide in her. Jonah's relationship with Beth doesn't involve Willow. She doesn't get special rights to information, especially when she's not sharing any of hers.

At the end of the day Willow is walking across the oval to the far school gate. Jonah is only a short distance behind her. Willow's ringtone cuts through the air. Jonah tightens his grip on his crutches and quickens his pace to lessen the distance between them. Is it Beth calling? The last time Jonah checked his phone there were no missed calls or new messages on his.

'Hey, how're you doing?' Willow pauses. 'Yeah, people are asking . . .' Willow says. 'I haven't mentioned anything . . . no . . .'

It's Beth, Jonah is sure of it. And if she's calling from her mobile, it means she would have seen his messages and missed calls. It means she is ignoring him.

Jonah's heart drops into his stomach and a feeling of hopelessness clouds over him. A lump forms in his throat.

As if Willow senses Jonah behind her, she turns around. Jonah doesn't look away fast enough so it's obvious he's eavesdropping. His cheeks burn and he's furious he let himself get caught. Will Willow tell Beth? Willow turns back around and lowers her voice so that he can't hear what she's saying.

She hangs up and puts her phone in her pocket then lingers at the gate.

'Hey, Jonah,' she says.

Jonah doesn't wait. Willow probably just wants to gloat that Beth called her and not him. Jonah squares his shoulders and doesn't break stride, moving straight past her like he has somewhere important to be.

Tuesday drags. There's still no word from Beth. Every time Jonah sees Willow tapping at her phone he knows she's talking to her. He resents Willow for it more by the hour.

On Wednesday a message finally comes in at morning recess.

Sorry I haven't returned your calls. I'm working through some things.

Jonah reads Beth's message over and over. Clearly he is quite low on the list of things Beth must be working through. He knows she has much larger things to be thinking about, but it hurts that their relationship doesn't rank very highly.

He takes a deep breath to calm himself and writes back.

Give me a call when you're ready.

He deletes it. She may never be ready.

Call me back soon.

He deletes it. Too desperate.

He looks to the sky. What is the right thing to say?

Hope you're doing okay. Take all the time you need. Let me know if I can collect class notes for you (or anything else).

Jonah reads it again, adds a red love heart and presses send.

He stares at the screen after it goes but nothing comes back.

When the final bell rings Jonah checks his phone. There's another message from Beth.

Thanks for being so understanding. Willow is collecting notes for me.

Of course she is. Willow is doing bloody everything. Jonah rereads the message. Understanding? Jonah understands nothing because Beth has given him nothing. You can't understand something you don't know a thing about.

Willow's laugh is so shrill that it pierces Jonah's skull. She's been Miss Popular since all this happened. People are lining up to talk to her, to find out how Beth is, and yet no one has asked how he's doing. It's like no one cares about him at all. They don't see his relationship with Beth as anything important. Willow is talking to Jamie Harrison, the captain of the football team, the guy all the girls swoon over. Willow tosses a blonde curl off her shoulder. Jonah scowls in her direction.

Warra gets up to leave and Jonah follows him. Jonah is so disgusted with Willow he can't help himself. He turns to Warra.

'Check it out.'

Warra looks at him blankly. 'What?'

'Fast mover,' Jonah says, pointing at Willow with his thumb over his shoulder.

Warra still looks blank.

'She dumped Sam a few days ago and look at her now.' Jonah says it loud enough for Willow to hear. She stops talking and looks up at Jonah. Her cheeks flush red and hurt flashes across her face. Her eyes flick to the door where Sam has just left the classroom.

Warra puffs a disbelieving laugh through his lips and shakes his head. He looks at Jonah.

'Dude, you're being a dick.' The way Warra says it isn't mean. It's like he's stating a fact.

Embarrassment singes Jonah as Jamie Harrison eyes him off.

Jonah turns and heads out the door and down the hall. He feels them all behind him, hanging back, whispering, giving him distance.

Fuck them.

Fuck them all.

He just wants to be alone, but someone behind him grabs his shoulder. He shrugs them off.

'Hey!' The hand grabs him harder.

Jonah whips around. Warra barrels forward, pushing Jonah into an empty classroom and slams him against the wall. Jonah tries to push him off but Warra is fierce and holds him.

'I know you're doing it rough right now, but you're being a prick.'

'Get off! You don't know anything.' Rage boils up inside Jonah.

'That's bullshit and you know it.' Warra's anger matches Jonah's. 'Don't you get it? It's just like when I nearly drowned. No one cared because someone else *did* drown. Just like no one gives a fuck that you *could* have been killed because Lucy *was*.'

Jonah stares at Warra. He does get it. And he's right. Jonah's been an angry prick since it happened. Willow's just being a friend to Beth. No wonder everyone is staying clear of him.

'If you want to hold onto Beth, or keep any of your mates, pull your fucking head in.'

Jonah doesn't know what to say.

'And if you speak about Willow like that again, expect a smack in the mouth from me.'

Warra holds Jonah's glare, then turns and walks away.

THIRTY-THREE
BETH

I put on a knee-length black dress and look at myself in the mirror. Dark shadows circle my eyes. I dab concealer around them and rub it in, but it just looks worse. My dress doesn't sit right. I've lost weight so it hangs in all the wrong places. I pull on a coat to hide it. I try on two different pairs of shoes before I decide on flats, then I take my gold hoop earrings out of my jewellery box. They were a gift from Mum and Dad.

Mum is being remembered as Lucy Miller. This is who the town knew her as. She will be cremated here in Australia this afternoon and in the coming weeks, when I get my passport, I will deliver some of her ashes to my grandparents in America.

It was Dad who called them to deliver the news. I didn't envy him having to tell them that their daughter, who they hadn't seen for seventeen years, was dead. I was sitting next to Dad when he called and could hear the pain in his voice. Dad sat, answering their questions, then retreated quietly into his bedroom. He must still blame himself for everything that's happened after all these years. After today, when I feel strong enough, I will call them and introduce myself.

I've had a tough week and have spent most of my time alone. I need it as much as I loathe it. Each day the distance between Dad and I widens. I know he's trying, but something inside me has shut down and he's letting it go. Normally we would eat together at the table, but I've been eating on the couch alone or in my room. One morning Dad got up and had a shower and looked like he was going to try, but by mid-morning he was on the veranda, staring out over the distance, miles away. Dad assures me that he loves me as a daughter, like he always has, but how does he know what that love feels like? He doesn't have a biological daughter of his own, just like I don't have a biological father. My accusations and blame jump around as much as my thoughts in general. I'm not sure how I'll go when I'm back at school tomorrow. I'm not the same person I was. I'm irritable and let out cutting remarks I instantly regret. The smallest things trigger anger and grief with no pattern or warning. A smell, a sound, a song, a place . . . everything reminds me of Mum.

Then I remember she is gone and my heart skips another beat.

Dad comes out of his room dressed in a black suit, his head clean-shaven. The pain in his eyes is palpable.

'Are you ready for today?' I ask.

'As ready as I can be. You?'

'All of my year is coming. Willow just texted. They're in uniform, but Willow, Jonah, Warra and Carly will be in plain clothes so they can sit with me. They're going to meet me at the gate.'

'You've got a lot of nice friends.'

I feel like everything he says is a justification of the choices he's made. Every time we talk I come back to the subject and Dad insists he did the right thing by not telling me anything, then we argue. But today I leave it. We can't fight today.

'I'm ready,' I say.

———

The street is packed with cars and there is nowhere to park. Dad pulls up in the middle of the road and police come to both doors. As Dad gets out, a police officer gets into the driver's seat. Two officers stand either side of me and walk with me as I approach the gate. Reporters take pictures and yell questions. The whole scene scares me. I had no idea our story was so public. We haven't been listening to the news and the media haven't been allowed on our property, so I've been spared from the spectacle we've become. Willow, Jonah, Trent, Carly and Warra are waiting for me just inside the church grounds. They each hug me and then I see that my whole class are assembled and waiting to the side of the building. They hush as I approach. I feel self-conscious with all their eyes on me. I smile at Audrey and a couple of other friends and give them a wave. I'm so overwhelmed that I can feel tears rising and my lip starts to quiver. I love these guys for coming. Dad takes my hand and we walk inside the church. The second big hush comes as everyone turns to see us. The hall is full and this fills my heart with a warmth I wasn't expecting. I smile but then my face crumples into a cry. I was worried people might feel deceived by us. I was worried they mightn't come. My crying is infectious and people start dabbing their eyes. Our identities were fabricated but it doesn't mean that the friendships we built over years were too. Where the fabrication of our lives begins and ends is blurry. This is what I'm struggling with.

Behind us Willow, Jonah, Carly, Trent and Warra stay close and follow us all the way to the front. Police are being discreet but I know they are there. They are in cars outside the building, in plain clothes inside the church and positioned at each entry and exit point of the hall. They say that they're not expecting Carlos to turn up today, but by the turnout I wonder if that's true.

Mum's coffin is on a stand at the front of the hall. I can't look at it. I'm not ready to say goodbye yet. I need more time. I need to know who she was before she was Lucy Miller.

Throughout the memorial service I learn lots about Mum. Nothing groundbreaking, just stories from friends I'd never heard before. I had never thought of her as anything but my mother, but when her friends and colleagues speak about her I realise she was so much more than that. She was seen differently to how I saw her. I love hearing it. I want them to keep telling the stories, but they can't. Dad is next. Everyone shuffles and a murmur passes over the crowd.

'Thank you for coming,' he begins. 'I realise that each and every one of you here has questions about who we are and why we chose to come here, and I thank you from the bottom of my heart for not asking them.'

Everyone laughs.

'But you deserve some answers,' Dad continues. 'Lucy would have wanted that, so here goes.' Dad takes a deep breath. 'Seventeen years ago, Lucy and I worked in law enforcement back in Chicago. Our lives came under threat due to an operation that went horribly wrong. We had to make some swift decisions. Beth was just a baby at the time and keeping her safe was our main priority. Every parent seated here in this hall today would understand this. Every parent in this hall would do whatever it takes to protect their children.'

The hall is still and quiet. Dad continues.

'It was not safe for us to stay in America, nor live anywhere in the world as ourselves. Once the decision was made we had to leave immediately. It was the hardest thing we'd ever had to do. Australia offered us what we needed. Like America, Australia has everything. World-class medical facilities and education, beautiful beaches, great cities, mountains, deserts and farmland. We flew over here and spent a few months travelling around to choose a location.

'One scorching hot day we were driving through the Hay Plains. We'd never seen landscape like it. Flat and vast horizons in every direction. We'd never experienced heat like it either. It was forty-eight degrees Celsius. For a while a truck drove on the road in front of us and we could see the indentations. It was so hot the road was melting. We were inexperienced travellers for such conditions and weren't even carrying water. Lucy and I started arguing about what would happen if our car overheated, or if our air-conditioner broke down — how long would we survive out there in that heat? Beth was still a baby and we felt so irresponsible for taking her out there unprepared. Then one of our tyres blew. We all got out of the car because it was too hot to stay inside. But there were no trees for shade. I turned the car back on so Lucy and Beth could get back in, but because we weren't moving and no air was going through the radiator, the car started to overheat. The ground was so hot I couldn't even kneel on it to change the tyre. I had to unpack clothing from the back to cover the ground. Things were taking way too long and by this time Beth was crying, overheating like the car. Lucy started to cry too because she was worried about Beth. Things were going from bad to worse and I lost my temper, which of course makes you work even slower.'

Gentle laughter and knowing nods from the crowd break up the tension in the room.

'Then a miracle happened. Someone stopped to help us. A woman with a baby. She gave us water, put Lucy and Beth in her air-conditioned car and provided a rubber-lined mat for me to kneel on. She grabbed her much-better-than-mine jack from the boot and helped me change the tyre. Finally, we were all on our way again. We avoided telling her our names that day, but she introduced herself and told me she was from Deni. Lucy and I were shaken by the experience and drove in silence for the rest of the way, but the whole time I was thinking, I need to see this Deni place. If people there are so kind and so trusting and so genuine that a woman feels comfortable to stop on the side of the road in the middle of nowhere with her baby to help an angry man my size change a tyre in forty-eight-degree heat, Deni must be a pretty special place. So we came here. We bought property and we stayed. And yes, we ran into that woman and baby again.'

Dad pauses and looks at me. 'It was Jodie and Willow McClean.'

I turn to Willow and look back to see Jodie sitting a few rows behind us. We smile at each other. I can't believe I'd never heard this story before.

'For those who don't know, Willow is Beth's best friend and Jodie has always opened her home to Beth like she was family. So although we had to leave our family back in America, we found a new family here. We were looking for somewhere to hide and build a safe and happy life, and we got that, but we also got so much more. We were welcomed into the community without hesitation. Lucy's birth name was Brendena, but that's the only thing about her that changed. The Lucy you knew is the beautiful person she always was, and she would be very touched if she were here to see the love and support you have shown Beth and I today. Thank you for your friendship, your kindness, for allowing us into your lives, and thank you for coming.'

Dad sits down and puts his arm around me. I take a moment before I stand and move to the podium. I adjust the microphone and clear my throat. A sea of faces watch me, silent, sad. Willow stares up at me. Jonah is beside her. He nods at me like he does when I'm nervous before a fight.

You can do it.

It brings me the confidence I need to start.

'Like you, I only knew my mum as Lucy Miller. A week ago I had no idea about her secret past, I had no idea just how much I didn't know. It's easy to focus on this, as it raises questions, creates uncertainty and doubt, and with that comes a whole mix of painful emotions. So for now I've decided to focus on the things I do know about my mother.

'Mum was generous, kind, funny and strong. During the last hours of her life I discovered how incredibly brave she was. She loved me, my dad, this town and her friends here. She loved the community spirit of Deni, the way people pitch in and help one another in times of need. She loved that it was a safe environment for me to grow up in.

'Family was really important to Mum and I know that it must have been terribly hard for her to have no contact with her parents and sisters in America. She gave this up to protect me. Until last week I thought Mum was an only child with no living relatives. This week I found out I have living grandparents, aunts, uncles and cousins. I am yet to discover what all of this means for me, just like I am yet to discover what my life will be like without Mum by my side. All I know is that I miss her and I will continue to miss her with all of the pieces of my broken heart.'

I pause for a moment to recompose myself.

'The Lucy Miller you knew is the true person she was. Thank you for welcoming Mum and Dad into your lives seventeen years ago, and thank you for coming to offer us support and to say goodbye to Mum today. I am very fortunate to have had such a great mum and I am very fortunate to have all of you in my life and to be able to call this town my home.'

There isn't a dry eye in the room as I take my seat. Dad hugs me.

Mum's coffin is white with a simple posy of pink roses sitting on top of it. There will be a plaque here in Deni for those who knew her and on that plaque she will be remembered as Lucy Miller. She came to this town as Lucy Miller and she died in this town as Lucy Miller. To everyone here who knew her, that is who she is. I am one of the pallbearers, Dad too. Together with a few others we will carry her to the car and then she will be transported to the crematorium.

We stand, move to the front and take our positions. On Dad's command we hoist up the coffin. Five of us place the coffin on our shoulders. Dad is too tall so he holds it at the right height for the rest of us. I try to keep my eyes straight ahead, but I catch a glimpse of Jonah out of the corner of my eye. He is stone-faced, standing to attention. I look back to the front, eyes stinging, and move with the others. As soon as the coffin is placed in the hearse, Dad guides me to a car. Police move in to help keep the media back and then we're away, moving in a convoy to the next stage of this awful process.

The next part is just for us.

After the cremation Jonah's on my mind and I want to see him, but police advise us not to go back to the hall so Dad and I go home instead. As soon as I'm at the house and in range I text Jonah.

I'm sorry we couldn't come back to the hall. Thanks for coming. Beth x

Nothing comes back.

I text Willow the same message.

Willow replies.

We all understand that you have to be careful right now. We all want you to be safe.

Then Jonah's reply comes through.

Take care x

I feel bad that I've thrown up a wall between us the way I have. I still don't know how to move forward from here, but I know that I want Jonah in my life.

I send another text.

I'm sorry I've been distant. Let me know when you can talk.

Jonah replies.

Any time is fine.

Police followed us home and checked the house like they do every building we enter. They've given the all clear and are waiting outside. Inside it's just me and Dad. We sit on the couch in silence. Now that the funeral is over I feel ready to talk about something I haven't been able to broach yet. It's like Dad's feeling the same and is waiting for me to start.

'I have questions,' I say finally.

Dad nods. 'I don't want to argue.' He looks exhausted.

'Me neither.'

He waits.

'Were you and Mum . . . I mean . . . she was with your brother.'

I'm not articulating what I want to say, but he understands what I want to know.

'I knew your mum before my brother did. She was sharp, good at her job, you couldn't help notice her. I was in a senior position to her, so asking her out was inappropriate. Then my little brother came to the team . . . It was instant between them. Love at first sight. I never let on that I fancied her too. I respectfully stood back. I'd never seen Tyler so happy. Then when you came along, God, he was over the moon. Talk about doting parents.'

This story is so sweet it warms my heart.

'Ty was already involved in the operation with Carlos before you came along, but he wanted to step out of it. He was still working undercover, but he was winding back and another operative had been introduced to take over in case we still needed someone in there after the bust. Ty's hours were all over the place and he couldn't stand being more than two feet away from you. The job was coming to a close, and he would have soon been living with you at home, but then everything went wrong. That night, his last words to me were about you. It was like he knew Carlos would go after you. He kept saying over and over, "Promise me, promise me you'll look after her."'

I'm a strange mix of emotions now. The warmth I felt a moment ago melts away. Dad's life has been one big guilt fest – raising his brother's child because he feels responsible for her father's death. I'm a giant, lifelong burden. The weight of this realisation hits me in the stomach.

'I think I've heard enough now,' I say. I stand and walk to my bedroom.

'Beth, wait. I haven't finished. You need to hear this.' Dad follows me to my door.

'Get out.'

'No. Let me finish.'

'I don't want to hear any more! I don't want to hear what a martyr you are. What a charitable guy, giving up his life to raise his brother's child.' I'm yelling now.

'I wanted to, Beth. I loved your mother. I love *you*.'

'Get out,' I scream. Tears track down my face. 'Get out of my room.' He steps back and I slam the door in his face.

I lie facedown on my bed until I'm all cried out. When I emerge from my bedroom the house is empty. There is no note. I have no idea where Dad is. I hate what I said. I hate myself.

I walk into Mum and Dad's room. The bed is made exactly how she liked it, the cushions perfectly placed. I lie on Mum's side of the bed, hugging her favourite cushion to my chest. There are two large cardboard gift boxes on the dresser. I know one is full of photos. I've seen it before, but I don't remember ever seeing a second one. It has broad black and gold stripes, rich-looking – an expensive or special gift.

I carry the box to the bed and open the lid. It's full of letters. The envelopes are different colours, grouped and ordered as though many writing sets were used one after the other. The envelopes are sealed and have letters inside. All of the envelopes are addressed to the same person in Chicago. Mum's mum. My grandmother.

I sit on the bed and look at them. I know it's wrong to open other people's mail, but is it wrong if they were never sent? Is it wrong to want to know my mother better? To know myself better?

I pick up one of the letters. I wonder whether I should call my grandmother and ask her if I can read it. Would she mind?

I hold the letter up to the light but the envelope is made of thick quality paper. I turn it over in my hand. The paper is smooth between my fingers. I breathe on the underside of it, hoping to loosen the seal, but it's so old it doesn't make any difference. I can't bring myself to rip the paper so I put it back where it came from.

I push the letters away and grab the other plain white box to distract myself. It's full of family photos. My life documented in images. Seventeen birthday cakes, seventeen Christmas trees. Starting and finishing school years. My first fish. First game of netball. First day in my karate outfit. A photo for every belt. Gun club, motocross, swimming. Sleepovers with friends – Willow stars in those, posing with no inhibitions, and the camera loves her. I puff out a laugh at the photo of me and Willow dressed up as mermaids. She looks like a real mermaid, lying on a rock, perfectly positioned for the photo, while I look like an awkward tetrapod. I put it aside to show her.

I trawl through the photos quickly – I've seen them all before – but then I stop. There's a photo I've never looked at closely before. I'm at someone's wedding, perhaps only four years old. I'm wearing a red dress with wide straps over my shoulders. My hair is golden but it looks dark brown in the photo. For as long as I can remember Dad's shaved his head, but before that apparently his hair was dark. I look like Dad. Everyone has always said so. I've never been told I look like Mum. Of course, now I realise I look like my biological father, Tyler. Apparently he and Dad were alike. In the picture I'm smiling at the camera. I don't remember the photo being taken, and I don't know who was behind the camera, but it wasn't Mum or Dad. They are in the background. The room is busy. A dancefloor is packed to one side, but Mum and Dad are sitting at a table together. Mum is smiling up at him and he is smiling down at her. It looks like they are about to kiss, or have just finished kissing. Their eyes are locked on one another. There is no mistaking what is captured in this photo. They are in love. They are happy.

I look to the door, my anger at Dad softening. The memory of my last outburst stings. I should have listened to his story, but instead I lashed out.

I walk out to the kitchen. I can hear the dull thudding of Dad punching the bag in the shed. I change into my training gear and go out to join him.

He keeps punching as I walk in. He's anchored the bag at the bottom so it holds fast. I walk around the side and pick up my gloves. Dad steps back. I punch the bag a few times. It feels good. I go harder. Dad steps back, takes a drink and mops the sweat off his face with a towel. He sits down, rests his elbows on his knees and watches me. I build up until I'm giving it one hundred per cent. I channel all of my anger and frustration and grief into every punch and keep going until all my fight is gone. I lean in and hug the bag while I catch my breath. Eventually I turn to Dad.

'I'm sorry,' I say.

He nods. 'I'm sorry too.'

'I've been a total bitch lately,' I say.

'No. Everything you're angry with me for – your thoughts are reasonable. I understand. I just don't know how to make it better.'

'How long was it before you and Mum, you know . . .?'

Dad smiles. 'From the moment we arrived in Australia we posed as a married couple, but it was one year, seven months, ten days and –' Dad pretends he's counting in his head '– about six hours before we were a real couple.'

I laugh and he joins me. It's nice.

'We both wanted to long before that, but it wasn't easy at first. Tyler was my brother, my best friend, your mum's partner. We were in a moral quandry about it for a long time.' Dad takes another drink. 'In the end, we both thought Ty would have given us his blessing. He loved your mother – God, I'd never seen him like that before. But his love for you was even bigger than that. It was bigger than anything. He would have wanted you to grow up in a happy family, with two parents who loved each other. Mum and I fell in love, in our own right, but we still weighed up what it would mean for you. You were always number one. In the end, we couldn't see any reason why it wouldn't be good for you too.'

'I feel really lucky to have had everyone looking out for me.'

Dad stands and walks over to me. 'Beth, it's so much more than just looking out for you. I love you with all of my heart. Like you're my own. You were my first priority too.'

I close the space between us and we hug.

And for the first time since we were found, since Mum died, I think there's a chance we might be okay.

Dad pulls back and has an intense look on his face.

'What is it?' I ask.

'About Carlos,' he says. 'He was here today, while we were out.'

My blood freezes. 'How do you know?'

'Stuff was moved around in my bedroom. Photos. One of the three of us was sitting on the dresser. When I left it was in the box.'

'Are you sure?'

'Yes. I alerted our guys immediately and called Carter but she thinks my mind is playing tricks on me. Told me to get some rest. Her theory is Carlos has already left Deni, and it wasn't enough to convince her otherwise.'

A chill passes through me. I'm totally creeped out at the thought of him being here.

'So,' Dad says, 'I've been thinking . . .'

THIRTY-FOUR
JONAH

Jonah paces back and forth. His ankle is still tender, but he can walk on it now. He bites the inside of his cheek. He hasn't had any time alone with Beth since that horrible night two weeks ago. They've been texting on and off since the funeral, but he knows what's coming. Beth will dump him today. He can see it a mile away. The thing is, he can't think of anything to say to make her change her mind. What's done is done, and now he has to face the consequences.

Beth comes into view, followed by Tim and Stewart in a car. She parks her bike and walks towards Jonah with the poise of an athlete. She's a little thinner than usual, but still fit and agile. She smiles at Jonah and it makes his heart melt, like it always does. She's incredible. She's everything Jonah's ever wanted.

'Let's sit in the park,' she says.

Jonah instantly thinks of the last time they were in the park together — excited, terrified and so naive. If only he had known what was to come later that day. If only he'd stayed away. Things might have been different. Lucy might still be alive. Everyone's lives might still be intact.

But wishing is pointless.

'How have you been?' Beth asks, sitting down.

Jonah takes a few seconds to answer. 'Okay.'

They both know that neither of them is okay.

'Things have got pretty messed up, hey,' Beth says. 'Thanks for giving me some space to work through it all. I know it hasn't been easy for you.'

Jonah nods. He decides not to volunteer what a pain in the arse he's been at school while Beth's been away.

'Carlos is still out there,' Beth says. 'Dad thinks he's watching us. It means we need a little more time . . .'

Jonah is confused about what Carlos has to do with them needing more time, but hearing those words is so intense that Jonah grimaces. He knows what they mean. He swallows hard and looks away.

'Yeah.' Jonah's voice catches. 'I figured you might say that.'

'It's complicated,' Beth says.

Jonah nods.

There's so much he wants to say but nothing's flowing. The words don't come so he lets Beth do the talking.

'Dad's not happy with the police effort. They're trying, but he's not satisfied with the result. He says we can't sit around waiting.'

Jonah guessed they wouldn't stay. Even if they don't go back into hiding, surely they'd go back to their family in America. Jonah has been running through all of the scenarios in his head.

'Probably for the best,' Jonah mumbles, not knowing what else to say.

The space between Beth's eyebrows creases. Jonah realises his response wasn't right but inside he's shut tight like a clam and he doesn't know what to say to fix it. He flushes red and this makes things worse. His eyes skitter around the park. He looks at anything but Beth.

'I'm really sorry all of this happened, Jonah. I really am. I know you're feeling awful and you must be wondering what the hell you've got yourself involved in . . .'

Jonah is confused. Is Beth trying to break up with him or not?

'But if you could just give me one more day.'

Jonah stares at Beth. Something catches her eye and she turns her head towards the shops across the road from the park. She sits up straight, her body tense. Jonah glances at what she's looking at. Beth exhales a long sigh of relief.

'I thought that old guy with the white hair was him for a minute.'

Jonah looks back at the man standing in front of the jewellery store. He's wearing dark trousers and a white shirt with the sleeves rolled up. A woman holding a shopping bag comes out of the store and they begin walking down the street together.

'Carlos looks like that?'

'Not really, just at first glance — the hair colour. Carlos is taller and heavier than that guy.' Beth leans back. 'I'm just a bit jumpy. I can't wait for all this to be over.' Beth and Jonah look into each other's eyes. 'I know we need to talk, Jonah. We have so much to sort through, and I want to, I just need a bit more time. Another day or so. I hope that's okay?'

Jonah doesn't understand but he bites his tongue. He's not going to add to her worries by being demanding or confrontational. If Beth says she needs more time, she needs more time.

'Sure,' he says.

He watches her walk away and is still none the wiser about where they stand. What difference will one more day make? Why didn't she just call him tomorrow?

All these unanswered questions are exhausting.

Thunder rumbles in the distance. Jonah looks up at the heavy clouds. The sky is bleak and menacing, like it's going to crack open and pour down at any minute. At least he has enough time to get to Little Echidna's and take cover before it hits. He texts Warra to meet him there.

At least storms warn you they're coming.

THIRTY-FIVE
BETH

As I ride, a cold spot of rain hits my cheek. I could get a lift with Tim and Stewart but I prefer to be outside on my bike. To the east grey clouds build on more grey clouds. Deni always gets lots of rain when it comes from the east. I hope it pours and washes this week away.

I stop in the street and look around me. Everything is still. No birds chirping, no wind. A motorbike on the highway shifts into a higher gear then fades out. I look back towards the park. It's empty and still as well. Eerily so.

Carlos, where are you?

I feel him here. Watching. Maybe I'm just on edge . . . I don't know.

I scan the park and look up and down the street at the buildings and cars parked along the kerb.

Lightning flashes in the distance and another spot of rain hits my arm. I get off my bike and walk it over to Dad's gym. I lean it against the wall before heading inside.

Dad is in the office doing admin. When he sees me he stops what he's doing and comes out.

Tim and Stewart walk through the door behind me.

Dad acknowledges them straight away.

'There's been a possible sighting of Carlos up north,' Tim reports. 'Carter's pretty confident he's flown the coop.'

Dad shakes his head. 'I just spoke to her on the phone, but he won't be up there. He's here. Somewhere close.'

'I dunno,' says Stewart. 'She sounded pretty certain it was him.'

'Why wasn't he arrested then?'

'We don't know. That's all she said. She thinks now that he knows, you know . . .' Stewart's eyes flick towards me. 'That his motives have changed. Maybe that's why he's shot through. She reckons they'll pick him up at an airport when he tries to leave, if not before.'

'I know, but I don't buy it,' Dad says. 'Carter also said she's cutting you guys back.'

Stewart nods. He almost looks apologetic. 'The threat level has declined, but we'll still be in town to make sure you and Beth are safe.'

Dad's not happy about it, but he already suspected as much. It's why we're putting our plan into action today.

'We need to know that if Carlos shows his ugly mug around here you'll call us. Please don't try to handle things yourself.'

Dad smiles. 'You guys seized all my guns, of course I'll call you.'

Tim and Stewart give each other a look.

'That's all we wanted to hear,' Stewart says.

We shake hands and say goodbye. As soon as Tim and Stewart are out the door Dad turns to me.

'Come to my office,' he says.

Dad closes the door and takes his seat on the other side of the desk. This is where Dad interviews people before they sign up to his classes.

Dad rests his elbows on the desk. 'I'm certain he's close by. He has invested too much in this for too long to just walk away now.'

'Well, this time we're ready,' I say. 'It's our turn to catch *him* off guard.'

'Are you sure, Beth? You don't have to do this.' Dad's worried about how I might be if and when I come face-to-face with Carlos.

'I'm sure,' I say. 'I want this to be over.'

Dad goes to a filing cabinet and unlocks it. He kneels down, pulls out the bottom drawer and reaches underneath. I hear the sound of tape ripping and he pulls out a Glock G29.

'Dad! You were supposed to hand in all your guns.'

He looks at me and pauses. He checks the magazine and then pockets it.

'I reported this one lost in a river years ago. I needed a spare, one the police didn't know about, just in case. We can't go into this unarmed.'

'I thought you were going to call the police for backup. You'll get into trouble.'

Dad looks away. When he brings his gaze back to me he speaks quietly.

'Getting into trouble is better than me or you losing our lives. If Carlos is here and if we do manage to lure him out today, we're going to need every bit of protection we've got. We'll call for backup, but I will not go into this without being armed. It'd be better to run and hide, to disappear again.'

Dad's right. I need him to be armed in case the police don't make it in time. I need him to be right there, ready.

THIRTY-SIX
JONAH

Jonah arrives at Little Echidna's Cafe feeling flat after his conversation with Beth. Nothing was resolved. He still has no idea if their relationship will survive after what's happened.

Lightning cuts through the sky and an ear-splitting clap of thunder follows. The storm is here.

As Jonah enters the cafe the sky opens up and the rain starts to pour down. He orders a drink and sits by the window, watching the squalls come in.

Jonah places his elbow on the table, rests his chin on his hand and stares out at the street. His conversation with Beth swirls in his head.

'Hey.' Warra appears next to him. 'Hello?' He clicks his fingers in front of Jonah's face. Jonah sits up.

'Oh, hey man, I didn't see you come in,' Jonah says.

'Obviously,' Warra replies, sweeping the wet hair away from his face.

The rain stops as abruptly as it started, but the thunder and lightning keep coming. An old man Jonah's never seen before comes through the door. His shirt and hair are saturated and his glasses are fogged up. He laughs, cleans his glasses on his shirt then walks over to the counter to place an order. His white hair makes Jonah think of Carlos. Jonah doesn't even know what Carlos looks like. He could pass him in the street and wouldn't know. He should have asked Beth more questions. How old is he? How tall? How heavy? Can he disguise his American accent like Lucy and Bear?

'Mate, I'm talking to you,' says Warra.

Jonah is pulled from his thoughts and looks at Warra.

'So what do you think about me and Willow?' Warra says. 'You think I have a chance?'

'What?' Jonah tunes in. 'You and Willow?'

'Yeah, I think there's something there.'

Jonah thinks about it. He should have guessed. It's so obvious now that Warra has said it. Of course he has it for Willow.

'I think you should go for it.'

'What about Sam?'

'Nah, he's already on with Charlotte.'

'Charlotte Murphy?'

'No, Charlotte Grace. Pretty much the day after Willow dumped him.'

Warra's face cracks into a smile. 'I hadn't heard,' he says. 'Hey, I thought you were catching up with Beth today?'

'Already have.' The heaviness returns to Jonah's voice.

'Oh, I take it things didn't go well.'

Jonah shrugs. 'She said she needed more time. One more day.'

'That's weird,' Warra says. 'What difference will one day make?'

Jonah's been asking himself the same thing. Why does Beth need one more day? Not one more week, one more month, or unlimited time. What's happening today that will change things?

Beth was so nervous. Her reaction to seeing that guy with white hair outside the jewellers shop was intense. She must know something. Maybe the police think he's in town. Maybe they'll catch him today.

A man with snow-white hair rushes past the cafe window. He's wearing a long black raincoat. Jonah notices that the man's left hand is bandaged. Why are there suddenly so many men in town with grey hair? Men Jonah hasn't seen before. He figures he mustn't look out for them normally. He must walk past people he doesn't know in the street all the time without even glancing their way.

Warra stands. 'No offence, man, but I think I might grab my gear from the gym and brave the storm. Make a break for home.'

Jonah stops staring out the window and sits up straight.

'Sorry, Warra.' Jonah realises he's been completely ignoring his best mate, but he doesn't offer any excuses for his mind being elsewhere.

Jonah watches Warra head back outside. Warra grabs his bike and leaves his helmet undone as he rolls out onto the road and disappears from view.

Jonah looks across the road and into the parklands. On the other side of the park are houses and office buildings, some with vacant space up on the first floor. Further down the street is a hotel that also overlooks the park. There are more vacant spaces away from the main street, in the same street as Bear's gym. Carlos could be here in town, watching and waiting. Everywhere Jonah looks he sees potential hiding spots. The hair on the back of his neck stands on end and goose bumps spread across his arms.

THIRTY-SEVEN
BETH

'I don't have to do what you say,' I yell.

'Beth!' I can hear him running behind me.

'Leave me alone!' I rush for the door. Large drops of rain splatter on the pavement as I take off. Water runs down the gutters from the last downpour and the sky is still dark. There's more rain coming.

'Come back!' Dad shouts.

I keep running.

'You will always be my daughter!' Dad yells after me as I turn into the laneway.

I head in the direction of the cemetery. It's on the edge of town. It will take me at least twenty minutes to get there if I jog, but I have to time things right. Not too slow that Carlos will easily catch up with me, but not too fast that he can't keep up. It gives me the creeps to think he's following me.

I reach the place where I have to leave the footpath and cross the BMX park towards the cemetery. This is so Carlos has to get out of his car if he's in one. I'm not to look around. I'm not to make him suspicious that it's a setup. I don't know if my mind is playing tricks, but I'm certain he's close behind me. Nerves wind up inside me and turn into fear. I hold it down so it doesn't turn into panic. I tell myself that Dad is close by too. He will have Carlos in sight. He will intercept him when the time is right. I just need to keep moving.

By the time I arrive at the cemetery, adrenaline is coursing through my body. I fight the urge to look around. I need to hide how stressed and scared I truly feel. If Carlos suspects something it will scare him off. The place is deserted, just as we hoped it would be. We didn't plan this weather, but it couldn't be more perfect.

The cemetery is fenced with wrought iron, but I note that it's low enough to jump if I need to. As I enter the gate, jagged lightning forks through the sky and thunder cracks the air. I slow to a walk as I go past the older part of the cemetery where the headstones are; huge slabs of intricately carved stone that I could take cover behind if I needed to. Then there are the tombs that look like single beds, again made from stone. In the newer part of the cemetery there are smaller headstones; plaques mounted on small rectangular stones that lie flat on the ground in neat rows. Some have bunches of flowers, others have cans or a stubby of beer sitting beside them, forever undrunk. I have no protection at all through this section. I want to run, but I force myself to keep walking at a steady pace.

I head for the trees. This part of the cemetery feels safer, more sheltered. I'd have a real chance of getting away if I was being chased. There are winding pathways, larger trees and shrubby secluded areas with bench seats. Rose bushes are scattered through the garden and tiny plaques are mounted on natural rocks. No one is buried in this section but people spread the ashes of loved ones here. Then friends and family have somewhere to visit and spend time.

I move along the pathway until I reach a round garden area hedged by dense shrubs. There's a wooden bench at the far end set against a low rock wall and a large stone sits just off the path. It's where Mum's plaque is going to be. Some of her ashes will be sprinkled here and the rest will be taken to her family in America. This is where I have to sit and wait, where Dad knows I'll be.

I look around, pretending to read the plaques. If everything goes to plan, Dad should intercept Carlos before he gets to the cemetery. Hopefully Dad will be here soon to collect me, to tell me the threat is over and everything's going to be okay. But my nerves are raw. I'm unarmed and exposed.

I'm wearing a ballistic vest, but it doesn't protect my head or limbs.

I walk over to the bench, sit down and study the rock, the trees and the garden. My eyes jerk towards every tiny sound. The rustle of leaves, a twig breaking. I'm listening so hard I don't know if I am imagining sounds or really hearing them.

I focus on Mum's rock. It's hard to believe part of her will rest here forever. It's a place where she will be remembered, a place where her friends can visit her, but I'm not feeling it. Maybe when her ashes are here and she becomes a part of the trees, the grass and the earth. Maybe then I will feel her presence.

The minutes tick by. It feels like I've been here forever. My anxiety is rising with every second. Dad has to deliver Carlos to the police before coming to get me. That could take more time than I expect. I could be here for a while. He said he was going to text as soon as he catches him though. My phone is on vibrate and it hasn't gone off yet, so I can only assume Dad is still in the process of arresting him.

The sharp mechanical click of a gun being cocked sounds next to my ear.

I freeze.

My heart thuds and my chest tightens at the sound. I know what it is instantly. There's no mistaking it. I grip the seat with both hands. What happened to Dad? It never occurred to me that he might fail.

I swallow and wait.

'Keep your hands where I can see them,' Carlos says. 'Stay right where you are.'

'What's your game this time, Carlos?' I say, trying to sound braver than I am, praying that Dad is on his way. 'Are you going to blow my brains out here in front of my mother's memorial stone?'

Carlos keeps the gun aimed at my head while he moves around the bench. He stands in front of me. He looks me up and down and shakes his head. 'Your father was a traitor.'

'Which one are we talking about, Carlos?'

He puffs out a laugh. 'So you're a wise-ass too, just like him.'

'Again, Carlos, you're going to have to be more specific. There's some confusion around the issue.'

'Your real father. The dead one,' Carlos says coldly.

Dad must be alive. I could cry with relief but I hold myself strong and give him nothing. I need to buy time.

'Well, I guess I'll have to take your word on that. I never got to know that one. I didn't even know he existed until you showed up and killed my mother, making me an *orphan*.'

My smile is pure hatred. I envisage kicking him. A spinning wheel kick, my heel connecting with his head. In my mind he crashes to the ground, unconscious. I've practised the kick a thousand times.

I know I can do it. A second of distraction is all I'd need. Maybe even less. Should I should try it anyway? If I have the element of surprise he might hesitate and I could land my kick before he pulls the trigger. He's hell-bent on killing me. I have nothing to lose.

'I can forgive your father for what he did,' Carlos says. 'He was just doing his job. He was good at it too. I was almost impressed when he revealed who he really was. He blew his cover, risking his life trying to save my son. He called for everyone to stop, to stop the raid. Your uncle, however . . . He was a cowboy and ordered everyone in anyway. He knew the risks, but he was in charge, calling the shots. So you can blame him for the death of your father. I think they call it "friendly fire". But maybe he had an ulterior motive. Maybe the *fire* wasn't so friendly . . .'

Carlos is spinning the story, trying to get a reaction, but I know my father. Not for a minute do I believe he would purposely harm his own brother.

'So why me, now that you know the truth? How is my death going to hurt my uncle?'

Carlos smiles. 'I admit I hesitated when I found out you weren't his kid. I decided to hang around and finish him off instead. But after doing my research, and your little spectacle in the street just now, I saw the real truth. He sees you as his daughter. He loves you like you're his, enough to die for you. Your death would destroy him like my son's death destroyed me. It's the worst thing I can do to him, and believe me, I know.'

'Eye for an eye, then.'

'Exactly.'

'What about you, Carlos?' I say, trying desperately to stall him. 'You'll never get out of this country without being arrested. You'll spend the rest of your life in jail.'

Carlos smiles. There's a wild look in his eyes.

'None of that matters,' he says. 'I plan on leaving here the same way as you . . .'

My blood chills.

This is a suicide mission.

THIRTY-EIGHT
JONAH

Not long after Warra leaves the cafe Carly walks in. Trent is right behind her. He goes to the counter to order. Carly sees Jonah, peels off her raincoat and sits down at the window opposite him.

'Hey, little brother. Where's Beth? Did you talk?' she asks.

'Yeah, she's with Bear at the gym.'

'Oh, Jonah, I'm sorry.' Carly reaches out to touch his hand. 'It'll take some time, but you'll be okay.'

Carly thinks they've broke up. Jonah wants to explain but he doesn't have the energy to deal with questions he doesn't have answers for, so he lets it go.

Jonah picks up a sachet of sugar and turns it over and over in his fingers.

'So what are you doing now?' Carly asks.

Trent sits down next to Carly. She's suddenly distracted by his presence and not so fussed about Jonah's answer. This suits Jonah just fine.

Maybe he should go. Do something to take his mind off things.

Staff call out a number. Trent gets up, goes to the counter and collects two hot chocolates. He gives one to Carly. They talk while they sip their drinks.

Jonah looks back out the window and watches someone cross the road. It's old Mrs MacKenzie who used to work at the fish and chip shop. She always gave Jonah an extra dim sim and potato cake whenever he ordered. She's wearing one of those clear plastic disposable raincoats but her hair is wet, like she got caught in the last downpour. The man Jonah didn't recognise earlier leaves the store and joins her in the street. They stand together, chatting. That's what Deni's like. Sometimes you go up the street for the paper and it takes you an hour because you see people you know and stop to talk.

The thunder is a constant rumble, filling the air with electricity.

Suddenly Warra skids in, riding way too fast on the footpath. Mrs MacKenzie looks at him with disapproval. Warra drops his bike and looks for Jonah through the glass. Jonah stands up, alarmed. Warra's eyes are wide. Jonah heads out the door.

'What is it?'

'Bear's in trouble. The police just arrested him. He was yelling and fighting like crazy. I think they found a gun on him.'

'What happened?' Jonah asks.

'I passed Bear on my way to the gym. He was in a rush, didn't even see me, but then Detective Carter and some other officers pulled up. Tim and Stewart and two others. Carter wanted to talk to Bear, but he said he didn't have time, said they'd have to wait. Then things got out of hand. One of the officers noticed Bear had a gun on him.'

'What! What happened?'

'Things turned to shit. When they tried to arrest him, Bear resisted. He even pushed one of the officers and ran off but the other three guys brought him down. Looks like he's in big trouble.'

'Was Beth there?'

'No, but Bear was yelling over and over that Carlos is here and Beth is in danger. That they had to go after her. He said she's at the cemetery.'

Jonah's heart picks up speed. Is this why Beth needed one more day? She and Bear were cooking up a plan to lure out Carlos and arrest him?

Jonah's mind is firing wildly like his heart. The vision of the man in the long black raincoat flashes through his mind. His hand was bandaged. Could that have been Carlos? He has to go to the cemetery to make sure Beth is okay. She's on her own and Carlos could be close.

'Warra, can I borrow your bike?'

'Where are you going? How long will you be?'

'I'm not sure, mate. I'm sorry . . .'

Jonah isn't lying. He doesn't know how long it's going to take to find Beth. Should he go to the police station first to see Bear, or should he go straight to the cemetery?

Warra goes to take off his helmet, but Jonah has already picked up the bike and is leaving without it. He pumps his legs as hard as he can and when he gets to the end of the street he turns left towards the cemetery.

Lightning flashes. The clouds have built up again and there's more rain in the distance. Fear and adrenaline course through Jonah. The cemetery is on the edge of town. Will he make it in time? He swerves off the footpath and cuts through the BMX park.

He reaches the gates and scans the grounds. The open space is empty. Where would Beth go? Where is Lucy's stone? Jonah leans the bike against the fence and enters the cemetery on foot. He makes his way through the headstones, never taking his eyes off the trees. As he gets closer he slows down to quieten his steps like Bear taught him at survival camp. Then he hears voices. It's Beth. There's no mistaking it, but who is with her?

He steps off the path and into the trees. He stalks forward, careful and silent, favouring his uninjured foot.

He crouches down behind the bushes and pushes through them until he can see.

He grabs his phone and switches it to silent. He shoots a message to Bear, Warra, Carly and Trent, just to be sure someone gets it.

At cemetery. Need help. Send police.

Beth is sitting on a wooden bench and the man Jonah saw in the street earlier stands in front of her, a gun pointed at her head.

THIRTY-NINE
BETH

I stand up. Carlos moves back, then raises his arm so the gun is right in front of my face. I'm a good five centimetres taller than him. If I get the chance I know I can bring him down.

'Sit back down,' he demands.

'No.'

There's movement to the side of us, then something connects with Carlos's head. A rock.

Jonah bursts through the shrubs and closes the gap between them. Oh my God, what's he doing here? What's going on? Where's Dad?

Carlos turns and fires. Blood spurts from Jonah's arm but he keeps running. His foot connects with Carlos's hand and the gun thuds to the ground. I pounce on it and fire into the air. Startled by the noise, Carlos and Jonah freeze.

'Don't move!'

Police sirens blare in the distance and thunder explodes above us. I zero in on Carlos.

'I could blow your brains out right now,' I say through gritted teeth. Hatred boils within me.

Carlos snarls, his cold eyes locked with mine.

'He did it on purpose, you know,' he whispers. 'He killed your real father. He ruined your life like he ruined mine. Your mother's too. He destroys everyone around him.'

I pause, the gun trembling slightly in my hands.

'Don't listen to him, Beth,' Jonah says. 'He's messing with your head.'

I glance at Jonah then lock eyes with Carlos again. 'Get on your knees and place your hands on your head.'

Carlos laughs.

'Do it!'

'You do it.' A large smile spreads across his face. 'You won't shoot. You don't have it in you. You're weak, just like your mother.'

At the mention of Mum my rage explodes.

'I'm not a murderer like you!' I scream.

Carlos sees his chance and lunges at me. With everything I've got I spin around and deliver a kick to his head. The impact is square on target — couldn't have been better placed. His neck snaps to the side. His body rotates away from me then falls to the ground. Out cold. I bring my left hand up to help steady the firearm and aim it at Carlos in case he moves.

Jonah staggers to the bench behind me and sits down. Keeping my gun pointed at Carlos, I move so I can see Jonah. His arm hangs by his side. He touches it and grimaces.

'Are you okay?' My voice is shaking. Jonah's sleeve is soaked with blood that's dripping and pooling on the ground. I lower the pistol and reach into my pocket for my phone to call triple zero. I tell them I need the police and they say they're already on their way.

'What happened to Dad?' I ask Jonah.

'Warra told me he was arrested.'

I swallow, trying to process everything. 'Do you know why?'

Jonah shakes his head.

My mouth and throat are so dry my voice is raspy. My hands have a tremor I can't stop.

'Thanks for coming,' I whisper. 'You did good.'

Jonah nods, managing the faintest smile. He's holding his arm at the elbow.

Firearms drawn, flak jackets on, police burst through the trees into the clearing. Carter leads the charge and Dad is with them too. I realise I'm still holding Carlos's gun. I take my finger off the trigger and hold my hands out to the sides. I turn towards Dad.

'Beth, look out!' Jonah screams.

Carlos is on his feet. He grabs me and pulls me in front of him, one arm across my shoulders. He forces the gun out of my hand then brings it to my head.

Dad freezes. 'Hold fire,' he roars as police raise their firearms.

'Hold fire,' Carlos echoes with a snarl. 'Isn't this ironic,' he says to Dad. 'You sound just like your little brother seventeen years ago. This must be what they call karma.'

'It's over, Carlos.'

Carlos chuckles darkly. 'Over is definitely what it is.'

Dad is quiet. No one moves.

Carlos starts to laugh. 'Not so gung-ho now, are you?' he says. 'Not when it's your kid in the firing line.'

'No one meant to hurt your son, Carlos,' Dad says.

Carlos steps back, forcing me to step back with him. The gun slips from my head. I don't hesitate. I twist my body, aiming a swinging elbow strike at his ribs. My momentum delivers the blow with force. I step back and follow through with a second elbow strike, vertical to the face. Carlos's head jerks back and I lunge away from him.

Gunfire rings through the air. Carlos stands still. Two dark red stains spread through his shirt, yet he stays on his feet. He raises his arm and his gun levels at my chest. His eyes are wild, his mouth a strange grimace. He staggers back one step and recovers his balance. He steadies his hand. I don't have time to wait and see if he can still pull the trigger. I turn, like I'm shielding myself, then move my weight back and leap, spinning backwards. I deliver a flawless bolley kick. My foot connects hard with Carlos's hand, his gun flying through the air. Carlos staggers back and finally falls to the ground.

The next moment the police rush past. Dad is by my side, his arms folding around me, bringing me everything they always have: comfort, love, reassurance, certainty. I curl my body into him and bury my face in his shoulder. He holds me until I break away. His eyes are filled with tears.

After seventeen years, it's over. So much damage was done, too many good people lost.

I turn to Jonah and he stands, steps forward and hugs me tightly with his uninjured arm. I tilt my face towards his and he closes the gap. My eyes close as our lips touch. Tears fill my eyes and any doubt about whether Jonah and I can survive what's happened dissolve.

'Everything's okay now,' he says, pulling me close.

———

When the ambulance arrives, Carlos is lying on his back staring at the sky. He tries to talk but can't.

He's placed on a stretcher and taken away first. Another ambulance is called for Jonah.

Even though Jonah insists he can walk, they make him lie down on a stretcher. The paramedics lift him up into the second ambulance and I hold his hand as Dad and I ride with him to the hospital.

When we arrive we're shown to a waiting room. I sit down and let the shock and sorrow engulf me. There are no tears. It's like the well is empty and all I am left with is overwhelming exhaustion.

But Bear is with me. My uncle. My strength. The man who raised me for his little brother. He gave up everything he knew to keep me safe, to give me the best chance of a good and happy life. And until now I have had a good and happy life. I realise with absolute certainty that although this man may not be my biological father, he's still my dad – the only dad I've ever known – and his blood runs through mine. We've lost so much, but we've gained something too. Today is the day we pick up what is left of our lives, we put the pieces back together as best as we can, and we live in truth.

FORTY
BETH, SIX WEEKS LATER

Dad and I check in our luggage. I pick up my carry-on bag and shrug it over my shoulder. We find the others in a coffee shop and sit down.

Willow giggles and her hand finds Warra's. I can see the zing between them. I smile and sit down beside Jonah, who wraps his good arm around me. Carly and Trent join us a moment later, loaded up with hot drinks for everyone. Dad grabs his coffee and wanders off to the bookshop.

We travelled into town on the train together, laughing and chatting all the way. My tears come and go – both happy and sad now. Today they are here. The love that I have for these guys is overwhelming.

The past six weeks have been hard. I miss Mum every day. There is nothing in my life that doesn't remind me of her. It's as comforting as it is painful.

Dad and I are going back to Chicago to deliver Mum's ashes and her letters, and to meet my family in America. I don't know how I'm going to handle the next few weeks. I don't know what I'll learn about myself, or how I'll change. Sometimes I feel like I'm split in two. In Deni, I am solid and familiar. I know who am I there. It's my home. But when I think of what America means to me I realise there's a part of me that's fragile and lost. I hope somehow America fulfils something that is missing from my life, something that has always been missing, even though I was unaware of it.

I look at my friends chatting excitedly around the table. They have supported me so much. They are as important to me as family. I notice Jonah is quieter than usual. We've spent a lot of time together since Carlos was arrested. He's been the warmest of lights in my darkest hours and I know I love him.

'I wish I was going somewhere,' Carly says. 'Somewhere tropical. I want to go to Thailand.'

'We should go,' Willow says. 'After year twelve.'

'Why don't we?' Warra says. 'We could do it instead of schoolies.'

'I'll be at uni by then.' Carly pouts. 'I'll have to get a job so I can pay for it.'

I love this plan. I love that my future involves these people. Friends I love and grew up with.

But who knows what will happen between now and the end of next year? Life can change so quickly. I've learned that the hard way. All we can do is try to live an honest life, true to ourselves, because what we do now and in the future has cause and effect. I may not be able to control what my parents did, but I realise that my decisions don't just affect me. The cause and effect of our actions flow on forever.

Everything is important. My relationships with friends and family. My relationship with Jonah. Things said and left unsaid.

I am the same person I always was, but I am also different because of the things that have happened. It sounds obvious, but change is the only constant thing in our lives and with it we change too. We learn and grow until the day we die.

I am yet to learn everything about who I am and who I will be in the future, but I know some things. I am American born, Australian raised. My parents were American born and raised and I have family there I am yet to meet. I hope visiting them helps me to find out who I am and where I come from.

Another thing I know is that it all matters. The big things, the little things. Everything that happened in the past led up to this moment in time.

Every second counts.

'Kennedy, it's nearly time to go.'

Dad's standing behind me, carry-on bag in hand.

I'm still getting used to my new name, but it feels good. When we left America and went into hiding, Mum and Dad's lives were stripped bare. I feel that by reclaiming my identity and returning to America to meet my family I am making things right again.

All I know is I am Kennedy Jane, I am strong and, whatever I find in America, I am going to be okay.

ACKNOWLEDGEMENTS

When writing an acknowledgements page there are many people I must include and then loads of others I want to include but can't due to the lack of space allocated. So many people help me in ways other than research, reading, editing, packaging, publicising and selling my work. There are too many to name, but to all of the bloggers, vloggers, friends, acquaintances, teachers, librarians and students who write to me or offer promotion, support and encouragement in real-world or virtual forms, I thank you. The power of your positivity is far-reaching, impactful and much appreciated.

Working flat out behind the scenes, and the person who makes all of this possible, is my brilliant publisher, Zoe Walton. Thank you for publishing my work and for giving me opportunities to chase my dreams. Huge thanks to my excellent editor, Victoria Stone, who I worked most closely with and who slogged so meticulously and diligently over every single detail of this manuscript. Heartfelt gratitude extends to the entire PRH sales and marketing team, who continue to package my work into beautiful glossy books and then do a magnificent job of publicising and selling them.

Also working behind the scenes and making things happen is my wonderful agent, Tara Wynne. Tara continues to support me and my career and

I cannot imagine navigating this industry without her.

For the fourth time in a row my work has been graced with a striking, eye-catching cover. Thank you to Christabella Designs for such exceptional work again this year.

Research is one of my favourite things about writing. I love the information I come across and the interesting people I meet during the process. Those who helped me research this book were Angus McKindlay, who offered expert advice on motor vehicles, Lucio Rovis, who gave his invaluable insight into witness protection, Lars Holden, who shared his extensive knowledge about firearms, and Jack Woodward, who answered all of my questions about karate. Please note that those who helped with research did not read this manuscript before it went to print. Any errors on any topic in this book are mine.

As with every book I write, I have a team of generous friends who read early drafts and offer superb feedback along the way. Thank you to Richard Duerden (who read numerous versions of this story and continues to support me from afar), Sam McKindlay, Joan Torney, Kerry Ferris, Rachel Broadhead, Sally-Ann Dillon and Lucy Keath.

Warmest thanks to my cousin-in-law, Kate Juracich, for supporting me, championing and promoting my work to her social networks and for throwing me an awesome book party at her beautiful home.

Natalie Durrant is one person who needs her own whole paragraph of thanks. Not only do I relentlessly discuss all things writerly with Natalie, but she also reads for me and looks after my kids when I am on a deadline.

There are a number of individuals and groups who offer continued and much appreciated ongoing support. They are Lionel Torney, Lynton Ferris, Roger Shaw, Carol Pirika-Shaw, Ivy Jensen, Lana Murphy, Tyler Harrington, Andrew Mole and all who work at the *Riverine Herald*, my fellow members of Deniliquin Creative Writers, Bronwyn Simpson, Kristine Parkinson, Darryl Ronchi and all of the staff at my local bookstore in Echuca. My gratitude extends to all booksellers of all outlets across Australia and New Zealand who stock, read, promote and sell my books day in, day out.

I have a group of friends who share every step of my writing and publishing journey – Rachael Craw, Trinity Doyle, Gabrielle Tozer, Rebecca James, Ellie Marney and Nicole Hayes. I can't succinctly put into words the extent of support and understanding these women give and what their friendship means to me, but I trust they already know.

Thank you to those who are behind #LoveOzYA for offering endless support to me and all Oz YA authors.

To my busy, robust family – David, Zoe, Tia and Eve – who do far too many things for me to list. Huge thanks to them for everything they do all year round. You guys are the best.

ABOUT THE AUTHOR

Fleur Ferris spent the first seventeen years of her life growing up on a farm in Patchewollock, northwest Victoria. She then moved twenty times in twenty years. During this time, Fleur sometimes saw the darker side to life while working for a number of years as a police officer and a paramedic. She now lives a more settled lifestyle on a rice farm in southern New South Wales, with her husband and three young children. Fleur's colourful and diverse background has given her a unique insight into today's society and an endless pool of experiences to draw from. When she isn't weaving this through young adult fiction, reading or spending time with her family, you will find her with friends, talking about art, books and travel.

Fleur's first novel, *Risk*, won the Australian Family Therapists' Award for Children's Literature, the Sisters in Crime Davitt Awards for Best Young Adult Novel and Best Debut Book 2016, as well as a YABBA in 2017. She has also written *Black* and *Wreck*. *Found* is Fleur's fourth novel for young adults.

RISK

FLEUR FERRIS

Taylor and Sierra have been best friends for their whole lives. But Taylor's fed up. Why does Sierra always get what – and who – she wants? From kissing Taylor's crush to stealing the guy they both met online for herself, Sierra doesn't seem to notice when she hurts her friends.

So when Sierra says Jacob Jones is the one and asks her friends to cover for her while she goes to meet him for the first time, Taylor rolls her eyes.

But Sierra doesn't come back when she said she would.

One day. Two days. Three . . .

What if Taylor's worrying for nothing? What if Sierra's just being Sierra, forgetting about everyone else to spend time with her new guy?

When Taylor finally tells Sierra's mum that her daughter is missing, Taylor and her friends are thrown into a dark world they never even knew existed.

Can Taylor find Sierra's abductor in time? Or should she be looking for a killer?

*'Gripping, devastating and terrifying.
The scariest thing is that everything that
happens in* Risk *is all too possible.'*

REBECCA JAMES, author of *Beautiful Malice*

OUT NOW

BLACK

FLEUR FERRIS

Ebony Marshall is in her final year of high school. Five months, two weeks and four days . . . She can't wait to leave the town where she's known only as 'Black'. Because of her name, of course. But for another reason, too.

Everyone says Black Marshall is cursed.

Three of her best friends have died in tragic accidents. After Oscar, the whispers started. Now she's used to being on her own. It's easier that way.

But when her date for the formal ends up in intensive care, something in quiet little Dainsfield starts to stir. Old secrets are revealed and terrifying new dangers emerge.

If only Black could put all the pieces together, she could work out who her real enemies are. Should she run for her life, or stay and fight?

'This one will freak you out and drag you in, all at the same time — Black is guaranteed to keep you up at night.'

ELLIE MARNEY, author of *Every Breath*

OUT NOW

WRECK

FLEUR FERRIS

Tamara Bennett is going to be the first journalist to strictly report only good news. Finished with high school, Tamara is ready to say goodbye to her sleepy little town and part-time job at the local paper.

But things take an unexpected turn when Tamara arrives home to find her house ransacked and her life in danger. What is the mysterious note her attacker wants – and why is he willing to kill for it?

A tragic boating accident five years ago holds the clue that could keep Tamara alive. But how can she find the truth when she can't tell who's lying?

'Fast-paced, action-packed and suspenseful, this would have to be the YA thriller of 2017!'

ANNIE, *read3rzrevublog.wordpress.com*

OUT NOW